ICE PRINCESS

Don't miss the beginning of
Alex and Samantha's story:

Ice Dancing

ICE PRINCESS

Nicholas Walker

AN
APPLE
PAPERBACK

SCHOLASTIC INC.
New York Toronto London Auckland Sydney

ISBN 0-590-47727-7

12 11 10 9 8 7 6 5 4 3 2 1   4 5 6 7 8 9/9

Printed in the U.S.A.   40

First Scholastic printing, February 1994

This book is dedicated to my son Alex

Contents

ICE PRINCESS

1.
Skating on
the Edge?

Alex Barnes and Samantha Stephens sat on the floor just inside the tunnel that led out onto the huge expanse of ice. This was where they always sat so they could see the other skaters but the crowd couldn't see them. Alex was watching with reluctant admiration as Carla Jeffrey and Wayne Jennings went smoothly into the last part of their free dance.

Samantha was leaning back against the wall, her eyes closed. She hugged herself and shivered. "I wish they'd get a move on," she said.

"Any minute now," said Alex. Both of them knew they had no chance of winning this competition, not against Carla and Wayne. They were years ahead of Alex and Samantha and had already qualified for the British Championships. Samantha shivered again.

"You all right?" Alex said, noticing for the first time.

"Of course!" she snapped. Her very vehemence

1

made Alex study her more closely. He leaned forward and felt her forehead.

"Hey, you're burning up," he said. She knocked his hand away.

"I said I'm all right! It's just this waiting."

"You're not all right," said Alex, getting to his feet. "Look, I'd better fetch Liz."

"You won't! We're on in a sec," she said. "It's just a bit of a chill, that's all."

"You know what your parents made me promise," said Alex. "Look, if you're not up to it we have to withdraw."

"Don't be such a wimp! I haven't come all this way to drop out at the last minute."

"Sam," Alex said, looking concerned, "there's plenty of other competitions."

"Samantha, not Sam!" she said crossly. Then the PA system in the rink broke into voice. "That's us — you can stay here if you want, I'm going." She scrambled to her feet and shot off to the ice. Frantically Alex dashed after her, only catching up halfway towards their starting positions.

A great bellow from the sidelines told them that Toby, Alex's best friend, was in rare form. Then the MC was reading out their names again.

They were both dressed in Indian costumes for their free dance: *Apache*. Alex as a chief, Samantha as a squaw. They had been aiming for second place but now all Alex was thinking was, "Could they hold the dance together?" Because there was definitely something wrong with Samantha.

The drumbeats for their music started and immediately Samantha's ten years of dance training took over, her tremendous self-discipline pushing her protesting body into keeping up with the music. A preoccupied Alex was half a step behind but by the time they had gone around the ice they were reasonably together.

The music hurried past and Alex settled down, but even so their performance lacked their usual *oomph*. They failed to grip the audience. When at last they sank to their knees in the dramatic ending where they entreated the sun to return, Alex was feeling disgusted with himself.

He took Samantha's arm and steered her over to the barriers. She leaned against them until their marks came up.

"We'll be lucky to hold on to third," Alex gasped quietly to Samantha. She wasn't even watching.

"What?" she said vaguely.

"Samantha, you look awful," he said. "I'll get Liz."

"No, I just need to sit down for a minute," she said.

"Your parents are over there, you go and sit with them."

"No! That's the last thing I can do — they mustn't see me like this," she said. "Get me back to the anteroom."

Alex half carried her up the tunnel and the minute she was in the anteroom she lay down on the bench and closed her eyes.

"I really think I ought to fetch someone," he said in a worried voice.

"Fine! You just go and get them — let them see me like this and guess how long my dad will let me go on skating," she said. "Oh, it's just a cold, Alex, you know how they affect me. If I can get through the award ceremony and into some warm clothes I'll be all right. I can pretend to sleep in the car so they won't notice."

Alex knew what she said was true. Samantha was the fittest person he had ever met but colds hit her like a sledgehammer. Only two years ago her parents had taken her out of dance college after a near fatal attack of rheumatic fever. He covered her with his anorak and fetched some hot chocolate from the machine in the corridor, but she didn't want it, just lay there shivering. At last, urged on by the PA system, they made their way back onto the ice.

A small podium had been set up on the ice with places for first, second, and third. Nobody seemed sure who had come second and third and they were taking a long time getting around to announcing it. At long last the MC came forward trailing a microphone.

"Ladies and gentlemen," he said. Then again, "Ladies and gentlemen," until the crowd quietened down. "In third place are Alex Barnes and Samantha Stephens."

Alex swore and reached for Samantha's hand. She leaned against the tunnel wall, her eyes closed. "Samantha?" he said.

"Uh? Oh yes, right." She took his arm and he almost had to drag her across the ice.

To Samantha the whole rink was an enormous echoing hole, the only reality was the familiar feel of Alex's hand on her arm. Dimly, as though from a very great distance away, she could see the empty podium. Empty? That meant they were in third place. What had happened? Surely they had planned on coming in second?

Alex halted her by the lowest position.

"Just there, kids," said the MC, his kind voice taking the sting out of their disappointment.

"Eh?" Samantha looked at him vaguely.

"Up there, my dear."

"Oh, yes," Samantha gave him a beautiful smile and collapsed onto the ice as if all the bones had been suddenly removed from her body.

Alex was left there alone, staring down at her.

2.
Black Ice

Alex sat in the hospital waiting area reading the posters on the wall. The door swung open and Toby came back from the cafeteria carrying a tray. He sat down beside Alex and handed him a plastic cup of hot chocolate.

"Are you sure that's all you want?" Toby asked, starting on a huge slice of lemon meringue pie.

"Yes, thanks," said Alex. He nodded towards one of the posters. "Have you seen that one about the dangers of cholesterol?"

"Cholesterol?" said Toby. "I thought that was an island in the Mediterranean."

Alex didn't laugh, just took a morose sip of his drink. Toby watched him anxiously. "Oh, c'mon Alex," said Toby. "You said yourself it was only a cold."

"Yeah."

"Well a cold's nothing to worry about, is it?"

"They brought her here in an ambulance in case

you've forgotten," said Alex, "with the lights flashing and the siren going!"

"Aah — that was just a precaution," said Toby. "Have some of this lemon meringue pie, cheer yourself up."

"No thank you."

"You're missing something. Considering the other garbage that cafeteria is selling they do an amazingly good lemon meringue pie."

"I tried to stop her, Toby," said Alex. "We nearly had a fight in the tunnel."

"You couldn't stop Samantha with a bulldozer!" said Toby.

"I only hope her parents realize that," said Alex.

"Well, here's your chance to find out," said Toby as the doors swung open again. Alex, who had already seen Mr. and Mrs. Stephens, scrambled to his feet.

"I'll be right behind you," muttered Toby. "And I do mean *right* behind you! I'll see you in the car park." He abandoned his lemon meringue and disappeared through the glass doors. Alex hardly noticed him go in his eagerness to speak to Samantha's parents."

"How is she?" he asked.

"She's all right, Alex," said Mrs. Stephens. "It was a false alarm — just a touch of flu."

Alex let out a long sigh of relief.

"Yes — no thanks to you," snapped Mr. Stephens.

"That's hardly fair, Donald," said Mrs. Stephens "It's not Alex's fault."

"Isn't it?" demanded Mr. Stephens. "Tell me, Alex, did you know she was ill before she went on the ice?"

"Yes, sir."

Mr. Stephens turned to look at his wife. "Satisfied?" he said.

She sighed. "Alex you promised to let us know if Samantha showed the least sign of illness," she said. "You know how dangerous even the slightest chill can be to her."

Alex was silent. He could only defend himself by putting the blame on Samantha.

"Well, you had your chance, Alex. You're going to stay away from my daughter from now on," said Mr. Stephens.

"She's my partner," Alex said quietly.

"Not anymore! She's nobody's partner anymore," said Mr. Stephens. Then to his wife, "Come on, Victoria, let's go home."

"Yes, you go and get the car, Donald," she said. "I'll be right with you."

Mr. Stephens gave an angry shrug but disappeared through the glass doors. Mrs. Stephens waited until he had gone then turned back to Alex, a more friendly look on her face.

"You're going to have to do as he says, Alex,"

she said. "I'm sorry, but we really can't let her skate anymore. You'll soon find another partner."

"You think it's that easy?"

She shook her head. "We're all going to have to make sacrifices. Samantha more than any of us."

"I need to see her."

"She's asleep, the doctor's just given her a sedative," said Mrs. Stephens. "He says she will sleep solidly for at least eight hours — perhaps you can come in with me tomorrow, if her father's not there, that is?"

"She's going to be all right though, isn't she, Mrs. Stephens?"

"Yes, Alex — this time." Mrs. Stephens went out the glass doors after her husband. She was replaced almost immediately by Toby. He went over to his friend who was leaning against the wall, looking upset.

"Were they mad?" Toby asked.

"Not really." Alex shrugged. "They're nice people, Toby. It's Samantha's fault, not theirs — and mine."

"How is she?"

"Asleep," Alex grunted. "Oh, she's going to be all right."

"C'mon then, if we miss the last bus it's a three-mile walk."

"No — you go, Toby. I've got to hang around a bit."

"If you're waiting, I'll stay and keep you company."

"Thanks, but I need you to drop in and explain to my parents. If I phone them they'll only demand I come home."

"OK," said Toby, relieved. "How long shall I say you're going to be?"

Alex shrugged. "As long as it takes," he said.

3.
End of a Partnership

It was two weeks later and the first time Samantha had been back to school. She was sitting in the Principal's study with both her parents.

"Well, as I've said, we are sorry to be losing you," said the Principal. Samantha didn't answer, just went on staring at the toes of her sneakers.

"Samantha," said her mother. "Your Principal is speaking to you."

"Yes," said Samantha. She stood up, "Can I go and get my things now?" Without waiting for permission she went through the door and shut it after her.

"I'm sorry about that," said Mr. Stephens.

"I suppose it's understandable," said the Principal.

"I'll go with her," said Mrs. Stephens, opening the door. She caught up with Samantha at the end of the main corridor.

"Hold on a minute, darling," she called.

"You needn't follow me," said Samantha. "I promise I'm not going to run away."

"Oh, come on, Samantha, there's no need for that," said Mrs. Stephens. "We're doing this for your own good."

"Where have I heard that before?" demanded Samantha. "Wasn't it when you took me out of dance school?"

"Yes, when you nearly died from rheumatic fever," said Mrs. Stephens, losing her patience.

"And this time it was a cold — just a darn cold!" Mrs. Stephens was so agitated, for once she didn't pick up Samantha's language.

"That cold put you in hospital," she said quietly.

"Rather a hospital than this prison you're sending me to."

"The Stoke Dameral School for Girls is one of the best private schools in the country."

"I've seen it. It's got a great big wall all the way around it!"

Mrs. Stephens went and put her hands on her daughter's shoulders. Samantha's face remained hard and unforgiving.

"You're sending me away again," she said. "You took dancing away from me and now you're trying to do the same with skating."

"You're not up to it, Samantha. You haven't the constitution to be a major sportswoman and you're incapable of doing anything half-heartedly."

"There is no point in doing anything half-heartedly!"

"There you are, you see," said Mrs. Stephens. "Look, darling, if you give me your word of honor not to see Alex anymore, and not to go off skating in secret then I'll speak to your father. We can see about sending you to another day school."

"What's wrong with Alex? I thought you liked him."

"I do, we both do. But he's a bad influence on you, and he's not giving up skating, is he?" said Mrs. Stephens. "Go on, darling, just give me your word — I know you'll keep it."

Samantha shook her head, "No," she said. "You stopped me dancing but you'll never stop me skating. I'm fifteen now and the most you can do is make me wait a couple of years." She turned away, her mother made as if to follow her. "Relax," said Samantha. "Like I said, I'm not running away." She looked back over her shoulder at her mother. "I don't have to, do I? You're sending me away!"

She walked off up the corridor, leaving her mother leaning against the wall with a crushed look on her face.

Mr. Higgins was teaching geography when Samantha knocked on the door and went inside. The class fell silent, nobody very sure what to say.

"Oh, er, Samantha," said Mr. Higgins. "Are you feeling better?"

"I'm fine, thank you, Mr. Higgins," said Samantha. "I've just come to fetch my things."

"Yes. I'm sorry we're losing you," said Mr. Higgins.

"Everybody keeps saying that," said Samantha. "Funny, a year ago no one even used to speak to me." She had to walk to her desk by Roberta Isgrove and to do so she had to pass Alex. The whole class could feel the almost tangible frisson between them, even though Alex was looking downwards, idly doodling in his exercise book. Samantha took a deep breath and made it to her desk without faltering. She started unloading her exercise books and other possessions onto the chair. Mr. Higgins stood watching, an embarrassed look on his face. The rest of the class was still silent, enjoying the piece of high drama.

"Um — Alex, would you like to help carry Samantha's books for her?" said Mr. Higgins.

"I'm not allowed to have any contact with Samantha," said Alex. Maxie Pearson made a rude noise that ended in a laugh, and Alex looked up for the first time and regarded him levelly.

"I'll help you, Samantha," said Toby getting to his feet.

"Thanks, Toby," said Samantha, loading him up with books. Suddenly everyone started speaking, wishing Samantha well. It was true, in the short

14

time she'd been there her relationship with the class had changed from one of being totally ignored to one of universal liking. Samantha gave Roberta, who was obviously upset, a reassuring smile.

"Let us know how you make out," Roberta said quietly.

"Of course I will." Samantha went to the front of the class. "That's it, Mr. Higgins. Thanks a lot."

"Well, the best of luck, Samantha," said Mr. Higgins, gravely shaking her hand.

"Yeah — bye everybody." Samantha opened the door and stood for a moment looking back over her old class. There was a lump in her throat. "You keep my desk free," she said clearly. "I'll be coming back to it."

4.
Liking
Each Other

Liz Pope, the junior dance coach, carried her big cassette player down onto the ice. A few people were skating around, bringing their training time to an end, for the dance club had the ice for the next hour and a half. She stared across the rink, then put a finger in either corner of her mouth and unleashed a most unladylike whistle. Alex, in the middle of the ice, looked up and came gliding over.

"Hi," he said.

"Hello, Alex," said Liz. "You've not been to dance club lately?"

He shrugged. "I didn't want to give Diane a chance to gloat." Diane had been Alex's first partner until they had fallen out.

"She's hardly in a position to gloat. She hasn't found another regular partner since Nigel went to America."

"You're not suggesting I partner up with her again?"

16

"I'm not suggesting anything, but I'm not sure what you're going to do," said Liz. "You thinking of going back to ice hockey?"

"No."

"So it *is* another partner we're looking for?"

"I don't know, Liz," said Alex morosely. "I'm not sure I could ever replace Samantha."

"You used to moan that she was too serious."

"She was right — it was me that was wrong," said Alex.

"Well, what *are* you planning, Alex?" asked Liz. "Carrying on moping around in the middle of the ice?"

"I thought I might try individual skating."

"You mean figures?" demanded Liz. "I can't see it — anyway, I don't teach figures. Can you afford one of the other coaches?"

"Sue said she'd help a bit."

"Ah, yes, Sue," said Liz. "She's your special friend, isn't she?"

"Yes, and that's all she is!" said Alex defensively.

"Don't be so touchy," said Liz. "So you won't be bothering with the dance club any longer?"

Alex shrugged. "I thought I might still come along," he admitted. "Keep my options open."

Liz smiled. "Good, I think dance is more your forte," she said. "You were working for your inter-silver, weren't you?"

"On and off," he said. "We were concentrating

more on the Juniors. Samantha was putting a new free dance together for then." He sighed. "Never mind, let's just see what happens."

The rest of the dance club were appearing in ones and twos. Most of them were extra friendly to Alex. Only another skater could appreciate the trauma of losing a partner.

Liz kept them to basic steps that night, fortunately for Alex because it meant they didn't do much pairing up. When the rest of the class disappeared, Alex stayed on and lost himself in the crush of general skaters who came pushing and shoving onto the ice. He found himself a clear space in the middle. Samantha and he had been trying out a more advanced turn that involved flicking the whole skate right around while still traveling in the same direction. Relentlessly Alex practiced the move over and over again, oblivious to everyone else on the ice.

"Hello, Alex," said a voice, and he jumped and turned, expecting to see Sue. But it was Diane.

"Oh — er, hi, Diane," he said wonderingly. It was the first time she had said anything to him, other than an insult, since the medal test when they had fallen out.

"Sorry to hear about Sam."

"Are you?" He didn't believe it.

"Oh, c'mon Alex. I know how you feel. It happened to me as well, y'know," she said. "Nigel and me, we were just getting used to each other and his parents up and move to America."

"Yeah, I know," he said. Then he gave a sigh, "What do you want, Diane?"

"Why should I want anything?"

"Because you're being nice," he said. "Only last year you deliberately ruined my skates to try and make Samantha and me lose our first competition."

"That wasn't me," she said.

"Oh, come on, Diane," he said. She was silent for a moment.

"You still won, didn't you?" she said. "I was wrong about you. You could be a darn good skater — you *are* a darn good skater. You rank higher than me in the club nowadays."

"It isn't going to work, Diane," he said. "We don't like each other enough to be partners again — remember how it was?"

"I was just playing with an idea," she said. "Look, we're both trying for inter-silver. We are both working for the Juniors — and we both need partners."

He sighed and shook his head. She gave him a rare smile.

"Think about it, Alex," she said. "We know each

other's skating — do we have to like each other as well?" She skated off into the crowd. Alex watched her go.

"That's the whole point," he said to himself. "Liking each other."

5.
The Icing on
the Cake

Toby came out of the storeroom holding a huge, square, cake tin.

"Told you we'd get one somewhere," he said in triumph.

"Look at the size of it," said Alex. "How many people are coming to the wedding for heaven's sake?"

"I dunno, we haven't really discussed it," said Toby examining the tin closely. "Hm, it should clean up all right."

"Don't they usually have three or four layers?"

"Tiers," corrected Toby. "She just wants one big square cake — I think she's frightened she'll be hidden behind it at the reception, else. Anyway, you can be more adventurous with the decorations on a single tier."

Toby and Alex were the only two boys in the home economics class. Alex had only chosen home economics as a subject to keep Toby company.

21

It was virtually a free period for him. Miss Talbot, the teacher, tended to ignore him. Toby was the star of the class.

"And your sister has seriously asked you to make her wedding cake?" Alex said. "I thought you couldn't stand the sight of her?"

"We've got this sort of love–hate relationship."

"You have?"

"Yeah, she loves me and I hate her," grinned Toby. "Anyway, it's cheaper than buying her a wedding present."

"It's a big thing though, isn't it, Toby," said Alex, "trusting you with the cake."

"Eh? Don't you think I'm up to it?" Toby was so taken aback he stopped polishing the inside of his tin.

"Of course you are," sighed Alex, who was well aware of his friend's capabilities. Toby lived his whole life in the world of food and was intent on training to be a chef when he left school. "I just mean trusting you not to throw it at her head during one of your arguments."

"She'll be employing me in my professional capacity," grunted Toby.

"Why aren't you doing it at home?" asked Alex.

"Oh, I like performing in front of an audience," said Toby.

"So do I," murmured Alex. Toby glanced up at his friend to find him gazing out of the window with a miserable expression on his face.

"How did the skating go last night?" asked Toby.

"OK, I guess," said Alex. "Bit lonely I suppose. I'd got used to being bullied."

"So you're just going to skate with Sue for the time being?"

"Yeah. She wasn't there last night though," said Alex. "She doesn't always go to dance class. She's a free skater really."

"You're not thinking of going back to hockey then?"

"No," said Alex. "Why? Do you want me to?"

"Nothing to do with me. It's just that I hear the hockey team needs a new right wing — your old position."

"Oh, I know. Maxie's already been sniffing around," said Alex. He smiled, "Only a year ago they said they wouldn't have me back at any price."

"They haven't won much since you left. Maxie's been talking about you a lot."

Maxie Pearson was the captain of the ice hockey team and he and Alex had never gotten along.

"Actually, I'm surprised you haven't given him a smack, the things he's been saying," said Toby.

"Oh, who cares about Maxie Pearson!"

"Well, I'm sure I don't. I haven't got a reputation to think of — apart from cooking that is," said Toby. "But you're supposed to be the tough guy in class, aren't you?"

"Not anymore," said Alex bleakly. "I'm a wimp who goes ice skating instead of playing a *man's* game, like ice hockey."

"Ah, so you *have* heard what Maxie's been saying about you then?" Alex didn't take Toby's bait, just heaved another sigh and went on staring out the window. Toby gazed at him in exasperation for a moment.

"Look, Alex," he said. "I've got to tell you — you've been a real pain in the butt this last week."

"Eh?"

"Everybody's noticing it! I know you've got a few problems but it's not the end of the world," said Toby. "Cheer yourself up, you miserable sod!"

"I'm open to suggestions," grunted Alex. "I've lost my partner. I'm not even allowed to see her! I'm out of the Juniors and I haven't even got anyone to practice with for my inter-silver. What would you do in my place, Toby?"

"Me? Oh, I'd cook myself a steak and potatoes and probably follow it up with a pineapple dessert. But you're different from me, Alex — more subtle," said Toby. "Tell you what, go and push Maxie's face in — or ask Roberta Isgrove out tonight, that should do it."

Alex grinned in spite of himself.

"Has Sam started her new school yet?" asked Toby.

"How do I know? I'm not allowed any contact with her."

"I'm not stupid, Alex," said Toby. "Of course you know!"

Alex glanced around to make sure he wasn't being overheard. "She was supposed to start a week ago," he said.

"I wonder how she's doing?" mused Toby.

"Oh, you know Samantha," said Alex. "She can handle anything."

In fact Samantha wasn't getting on at all well. At that moment she was hiding in the locker room. Most of the girls in her year were on a cross-country run and Samantha was using the time to work in her sketch pad.

There was the sound of someone gasping and Samantha immediately slid her book into her bag. Marella, the sports captain, came struggling into the room. When she saw Samantha she immediately straightened up and jogged the last few steps. Samantha waited; she didn't make friends quickly and she knew that Marella was never going to be top of her list when she did.

"Goofing off again?" rapped Marella.

"That's right, Marella," said Samantha.

"You're a bit of a wimp, aren't you?" said Marella. "We don't encourage that sort of thing here, you know."

"I didn't see the point of going for a five-mile run in a muddy field," said Samantha.

"Point?" demanded Marella. "The point is that I'm in training for the county championships and most of the other girls believe in keeping fit."

"*Fit?*" Samantha couldn't keep the laughter out of her voice.

"Yes, fit!" snapped Marella.

"How would you know what fit was?"

"And I suppose you know all about it, do you?"

"That's right," said Samantha levelly. "I've been a professional athlete for the last ten years."

"Athlete? You were a dancer!"

"Same thing," said Samantha, getting to her feet. She gave a deliberate yawn. Then, just when Marella looked as if she was about to explode, a freshman put her head around the door.

"Samantha Stephens?"

"That's me, unfortunately," said Samantha. "Not Tom Cruise on the phone again?"

"Mrs. Rollinson wants you."

"Oh, good news," said Samantha, picking up her bag.

"Perhaps she wants to make you sports mistress?" suggested Marella.

"It wouldn't be such a bad idea at that," said Samantha. "I might show you one day."

Mrs. Rollinson, the Principal of Stoke Dameral School for Girls, was a large friendly woman, but she was still a principal. She waved Samantha to a seat and studied her carefully for a minute. Samantha didn't much care. All her life she had been pushed and bullied by ballet teachers, jazz instructors, choreographers, and the like — all of them much tougher than this Mrs. Rollinson.

"Well, Samantha," she said at last. "How are you getting along?"

"I'm all right. I don't know about you," said Samantha.

"Don't be impertinent!"

"It's a failing of mine. I would expel me if I were you."

Mrs. Rollinson sighed. "I am aware that you are here very much under protest," she said more gently. "But even so you are not trying to make the best of your situation, are you, Samantha?"

The Principal was being nice and this didn't suit Samantha's purposes at all, so she gazed past her and stared at the heavy black curtains that covered the window.

"I'm not planning on being here long," she muttered.

"Your parents think otherwise."

Samantha didn't answer, she sat there wondering if the curtains were really velvet.

"They say you haven't written home yet."

"I can't afford a stamp on the allowance you give to me."

"My instructions are that your money is to be

strictly controlled," said Mrs. Rollinson. "I'm not saying I agree with it, but your father assures me that if you get hold of any money you will put it towards a new pair of ice skates."

Samantha met her eyes. "He smashed my old ones — with a hammer. Smashed them! Did he tell you that?"

"Yes, and he told me why. Samantha, I'm not going to argue the rights and wrongs of your case. All that matters is that you have been sent here to keep you away from ice skating and to prevent you having any contact with this boyfriend of yours."

"He's not my boyfriend! He's my skating partner."

"*Was* your skating partner."

"Is!" said Samantha defiantly. "Nothing any of you can do can change that. Only Alex and I can break up our partnership."

"That's as may be, but your life here will only get more difficult if you refuse to cooperate."

"More difficult! You tell me how it could get worse?" demanded Samantha. "I'm not allowed out without an escort! I can't have any magazines unless you see them first! I get a few dollars a week allowance — my television's censored! I'm not even allowed any letters without them going through you first! I thought this was supposed to be a school, not Gestapo Headquarters!" Samantha's eyes filled with tears and she brushed them angrily away and went back to the curtains.

Mrs. Rollinson was silent for a moment. "When you prove you can be trusted, I will be only too happy to relax the restrictions on you," she said.

"Well, I'll tell you now," said Samantha. "I can't be trusted! My parents made me give up dance — there's no way they're going to get me to give up skating."

"Well, you really can't complain about the limitations we put on your freedom," said Mrs. Rollinson reasonably. "And if you go on cutting class and sports, you're only going to spend every night in detention. Samantha, the other girls are happy here. Our waiting list is one of the longest in the country. You're only here because of your special circumstances. You'll soon settle down and get over this silly obsession of yours. It's all happened before."

"I cut class because I'm miles behind the rest of them," said Samantha. "And I cut sports because it's supposed to be bad for my heart — or didn't you know? That's why I'm here!"

"You're here because you can't be trusted not to exercise to excess. Your doctor assures me that, as long as you haven't any kind of chest infection, sports won't hurt you."

"I'm not over my cold yet," said Samantha.

"And still I'm told you go running every morning and spend every lunchtime riding up and down the driveway on that funny bike of yours."

"The secret policeman on the gate won't let me through."

"The caretaker has been instructed that you're confined to the premises." Mrs. Rollinson opened Samantha's file, which lay on the desk in front of her. "Now, Samantha, you have got to take part in at least one sport. It's part of the national curriculum and one of the school's most important rules. And I don't mean cycling or running on your own — the idea of sport is to participate."

"I don't think you have to tell me that," said Samantha, meeting her eyes again.

"No, no, of course not." Mrs. Rollinson regarded her levelly. "Well, it's up to you, Samantha, either you choose a sport or I'll choose one for you."

Samantha sighed. "If I must, I don't mind swimming I suppose," she said grudgingly. The Principal was delighted.

"There you are, swimming," she said writing it down in Samantha's file. "I told you, you'll soon start fitting in with the other girls."

6.
Skating into Danger

Mrs. Barnes put a plate of scrambled eggs in front of Alex, then sat down opposite him. It was Monday morning and Alex was in a hurry because he had his paper route to get through before school. His mother had a worried look on her face.

"I don't know about this at all, Alex," she said. "You know your father thinks you spend too much time at the rink as it is."

"I know, but if you have a word with him he'll come around," said Alex.

"We thought you'd be skating less since Samantha went away," said Mrs. Barnes. "Now you want to skate two mornings a week as well!"

"I don't see the problem. The school says I can go in late on Tuesdays and Thursdays, as I've got free periods then anyway," said Alex. "The Principal understands, why can't you?"

"I do understand, Alex, so does your father

31

really. It's just that — well, your exams are this year, you know."

"But the two mornings aren't going to affect my exams. All I'll miss is assembly."

"Why does it have to be this new place? What's it called again?"

"The Coliseum Sports Arena," supplied Alex. "Because our rink is only open to coaches at that time of the morning, and I can't afford a coach. Anyway, the Coliseum is brilliant — and the Juniors is being held there. I need to adjust to the ice."

"What about Sue? Has the bank agreed to her going into work late two mornings a week?"

"Yes, Mom. She's been doing it for a year now," said Alex. "Firms do that sort of thing. They like the publicity when you become famous."

"When!" said Mrs. Barnes. "Oh well, I suppose, if Sue's going to be with you, it'll be all right."

"Thanks, Mom," said Alex. He put down his knife and fork and went around the table to give her a kiss. "Why is it you trust Sue and not me?"

"Because, in the five years she was your baby-sitter, she never let us down once."

"And I have?"

"Not yet," said Mrs. Barnes with a sigh.

It was Thursday before Alex found himself being driven into the Coliseum's enormous car park.

"Look at this place," he said in awe. "It's unbelievable."

"I forgot you hadn't seen it before," said Sue. She parked her battered car in an empty slot by the main door. "Wait until you see the ice. There are two rinks, a main one and a smaller practice rink. There's even an outside one, though that's mainly used for hockey."

They climbed out of the car and Sue led Alex down glass-covered passageways and through inner courtyards and fountains, until he thought he'd never find his way out again. At last she stopped and pointed.

"The men's locker room is down there, just follow the signs," she said. "Keep going and you'll come to the rink."

"Cheers — will your coach be here already?"

"Yes, he starts at six. I've got half an hour with him at seven thirty," she said, glancing at her watch. "If I don't manage to see you before, try and be back at the car by nine, will you?"

"Sure," said Alex. He watched her hurry away in the opposite direction and stood there for a moment feeling lonely. Then he took a deep breath, picked up his sports bag and went down the corridor to the locker room.

Ten minutes later he found himself gazing out across one of the most beautiful rinks in Europe. A few coaches were putting individual students through their paces but there was so much room he hardly noticed them. He could see Sue over on the other side, on the smaller rink.

Warily he stepped out onto the ice — almost afraid to mark it — and let his momentum carry him along. Every rink has a different feel to it: the atmosphere, the lighting, even the surface is different, and Alex glided around, getting a taste of it all. He glanced at his watch and made his way back to where he'd left his sports bag. He stopped by the entrance to the tunnel and a small figure stepped out of the shadows and put her arms around him. She hugged him so hard it hurt.

"Hey, what is this?" he demanded. "Not getting all sentimental, surely?"

"Sorry," she said, letting go of him.

"You're crying," he said.

"No!" said Samantha, hurriedly brushing a sleeve across her eyes. "It's just the cold in here."

"Yes, and you're not used to that, are you?" he said with a broad grin.

"Shut your face, Alex Barnes," she said charmingly. "I've just been a bit lonely — OK?"

"So have I, Samantha," he said more seriously. "Your letter didn't say much — won't anybody miss you?"

"Ah, there are four different pools here, they'll just think I'm in one of them," she said. "Have you got my skates?"

"Sure." He unzipped his sports bag and produced Samantha's Gelati Golds, her best skates that she always kept at the rink, and which her parents didn't know anything about. She handled them reverently, putting them on with the ease of long practice, then pushed herself onto the ice letting out a long breath of ecstasy.

"Oooh, freedom," she said.

"Yeah, I know how you feel," he said, joining her and gliding around the rink. "This is the first time I've come alive in weeks — how's school?"

"Awful, like something out of the Chalet school books," she said. "I keep thinking I'm in Colditz, only there's no escape committee."

"But you're allowed out for swimming twice a week?"

"Yes — I know it's not enough," she said. "At least it gives us a chance to see each other." Then she added hurriedly, "To keep in practice, I mean."

"We aren't going to win many competitions on two mornings a week though, are we?"

"Just let my dad calm down a bit, then I'll get to work on him," she said. "I'm going to try and get thrown out of school."

"Oh, that'll make him calm down," said Alex.

"It'll be all right as long as I'm careful about it," said Samantha. "I don't mean burn the school down or anything. I thought I'd just not fit in, you know, with the work and everything."

"Don't you think they've considered that?"

"Hm, that's the trouble," she sighed. "Anyway, I do a fair bit of static training when I can. What about you?"

"I'm doing three, four nights a week, now two mornings."

"What about Saturdays?"

"No way! I've only ever skated on Saturdays just before a competition," said Alex.

"But Alex, you've got to skate Saturdays!" said Samantha. "I've promised Monica."

"Who the hell's Monica?"

"Just a girl I've been giving a bit of coaching to for the last six months," said Samantha. "I told her you'd look after her for a bit — she's usually there about seven."

"Samantha!" Alex started to protest, "I go out Saturday nights."

"Well, I'll leave it up to you," said Samantha sweetly. Then she deliberately changed the subject. "Who's doing your paper route while you're here?"

"Toby."

"Toby?" She was so surprised one skate got away from her. "You've never got Toby on a bike?"

"He's none too happy about it, but I need the cash," said Alex. "How's your money situation?"

"Oh, me, I get roughly enough to buy a packet of mints each week," she said.

"How do you manage the entrance money here?"

"The school pays it — one entry fee covers everything: swimming, skating, playing squash — there's even a bowling green."

"Well, we should be warmed up enough," said Alex. "We'd better run through the inter-silver dances, hadn't we?"

"Yes, we can't waste time flapping our gums if we've only got two mornings together," said Samantha. Alex grinned at this. Samantha wouldn't let him waste time "flapping his gums" even if they skated seven days a week. They started off going through the three dances for the medal test, skating almost without a pause, really working at it. Half an hour later they halted at the far end, both of them panting for breath.

"Your timing's a bit off," he gasped.

"My timing's never off!" she said. "My skating might be a little rusty, my balance might have suffered — but *never* my timing."

"You're saying it's me?"

"Oh, it's you!" she said adamantly. Alex knew better than to argue. When it came to the dance side, she was the expert.

"Hm, I think I might've adjusted to Sue," he said.

"Don't you dare!"

"Look, Sam — "

"Samantha!" she corrected him crossly. He didn't mind. He knew Samantha didn't like people really close to her shortening her name.

"Yes — look, you're sure you can't get any more time off?"

"I've told you, it's a miracle I've managed this much."

"Don't you get any free time? Even prisoners get let out on parole."

"Sure, Saturday afternoon. All the high school's allowed out as long as you say where you're going," she said. "Except — that is — for me! I've got to prove myself first." She pulled a face. "I can either join one of the organized parties or talk a prefect into coming out with me."

"Oh," he said, taking her arm and pushing off again. They automatically started running through the dances again only taking it easier this time. "Look, it's around here, one-two, then turn, three-four." He guided her past the barriers and glanced at her. "It isn't going to work," he said.

"What isn't?" she demanded, bringing him to a halt.

"We need the two mornings just to work for the inter-silver," he said. "There's no way we can enter for competitions as well."

"We've got to. They're the whole reason for skating."

"And you're talking about changing our free dance as well?"

"Yes. *Apache*'s old now. Everybody's seen it and anyway the music's no longer on the charts."

"Well, OK then, try this on for size," he said. "Just say we manage to put a new free together, and just say we enter the Juniors — it's held on a Saturday — how are you planning on escaping, eh?"

She gave him a sweet smile. "Just trust me, Alex," she said. "I'll think of something." They started off again. Alex was silent for a full circuit of the ice.

"That's exactly what I'm afraid of," he said darkly.

7.
Private Dancer

"I'm sorry to have to tell you that Samantha isn't really settling down at all," said Mrs. Rollinson. Samantha's parents, sitting the other side of her desk, looked at one another. Mrs. Stephens gave a sigh.

"How do you mean? Not settling in?"

"Well, I know she's only been here four weeks but she hasn't made any friends at all. She avoids all the sports lessons — we virtually had to force her to take up swimming. And, as for work, well . . ." The Principal consulted Samantha's file on the desk in front of her. "Samantha does the very minimum amount of work she can get away with. She spent every evening last week in detention because she won't do her homework. And, just these last few days, she's taken to cutting classes altogether."

"She's not been allowed out of school, has she?" asked Mr. Stephens.

"Only when she's been strictly supervised — as

you instructed. I'm not saying she's particularly bad. It's more a form of passive resistance."

"She wants you to expel her," said Mr. Stephens.

"Oh, Donald," put in Mrs. Stephens.

"Of course she does," said Mr. Stephens. "Mrs. Rollinson, are you saying you can't handle her?"

"Not at all, Mr. Stephens. We've had a lot worse girls here than Samantha. It's just that it's difficult to discipline the girl: She doesn't seem to care if she's put into detention. We can't stop her outside leave because she doesn't get any. We can't even put a levy on her allowance because she only gets a few dollars a week."

"Yes, we do see your difficulty," said Mrs. Stephens.

"You know she still hasn't written to us?" said Mr. Stephens to the Principal.

"Oh, dear. I am sorry," said Mrs. Rollinson. "I ordered her to do so. I even issued her some first-class stamps — there's little else I can do. I don't see how we can force her to write letters."

"Who is she writing to then?" said Mr. Stephens. "Alex?"

"No, I've spoken to his mother," said Mrs. Stephens. "She's keeping an eye on his mail."

"We'd better have a word with her," said Mrs. Stephens. "See what she's got to say for herself."

"Yes, she should be here by now. Ah!" said the Principal as there came a tap on the door. "Come

41

in," she said and Mary Boswell, the Head Girl, came into the room.

"I'm sorry, Mrs. Rollinson," she said. "We've looked everywhere."

"You mean you can't find her?" demanded Mrs. Rollinson.

"I'm sorry, no."

"She must be on the school grounds?"

"I'm sure she is. I've had a word with the caretaker and he says no one's gone out of the gates this morning," said Mary. "And I've got all the prefects looking, but the trouble is there are so many places *to* look."

"All right then, Mary." Mrs. Rollinson dismissed her. With an extremely embarrassed expression on her face she cleared her throat and said, "I'm sorry about that Mr. and Mrs. Stephens. It really is most unusual that we are unable to locate one of our girls."

"It's not your fault, Mrs. Rollinson," said Mr. Stephens standing up. "She's just punishing us for sending her away."

There was tension of another kind back at Mount's Park School. At least in the home economics room. Everybody was hovering around the big end oven. Even the cooking teacher, Miss Talbot, had a preoccupied expression on her face. The only person who didn't seem concerned was Toby. He was sitting over on the far side of the room, calmly reading a book on cake decoration. Alex was sitting opposite, swinging his legs.

"How long now?" Alex asked.

"Eh? Oh, the timer will tell us. I don't know," said Toby absently. "I think I might try a treble trellis."

"Good idea," said Alex, who had no idea what his friend was talking about. "Any more mail for me?"

"I already told you, no!" said Toby. "C'mon Alex, you've had one letter this week and you're seeing her Thursday morning."

"Ssh." Alex looked around nervously. "Keep it down, will you?"

"Aah, there's no one listening," said Toby. "Look, I promise you, if I had a letter I wouldn't forget to give it to you. It's about the only thing that cheers you up just lately."

"Oh." Alex unwrapped a piece of chewing gum and put it in his mouth. He handed Toby a piece. "I thought I'd been OK the last couple of weeks," he said.

"You've been better since you've been seeing her mornings, yes," said Toby. "But it's the days in between that you go around biting people's heads off."

"You don't know what it's like, Toby," said Alex. "Nothing ever goes wrong for you."

"Nothing ever goes wrong for me?" Toby repeated incredulously. "What about last week, when my soufflé failed to rise? I know all about heartache, believe me!" Alex grinned in spite of himself.

"How's the paper route coming on?" he asked.

"I'd rather not talk about it," said Toby, then immediately did so. "You never said anything about the dog at Holland Terrace."

"What? Tegs? He's as gentle as a lamb."

"Yeah? Well, he chewed the saddle off your bike yesterday morning."

"Oh great, couldn't you be more careful?"

"I am exceedingly sorry. I must try harder." Toby glanced up at his friend. "You have remembered that we're going to see a film on Saturday night?"

"Oh," said Alex. "We may have a problem there."

"A problem?" demanded Toby. "What d'you mean a problem? You said that if I did your paper route two mornings a week you'd pay for the movies, and something to eat afterwards!"

"I'm sorry, Toby, I can't make Saturday."

"You do realize that we are the only two people left in the western world who haven't seen *Cloak and Dagger*?" demanded Toby.

"*Cloak and Dagger*? Oh, that film everybody's talking about?" said Alex. "Make it another night, Toby. I really have something I've got to do."

"Don't act all mysterious with me," said Toby. "You're going to the rink!"

44

"Yeah, well — I've got to do something for Samantha, look after someone she's been teaching."

Toby sighed. "You'd just better mean it about another night, Alex Barnes," he said. "Or I might accidentally drop your newspapers in the — " Toby broke off as the timer finally went, making everybody but him jump. Reluctantly he stretched, yawned, then after a decent interval strolled across the room.

"Give me some space," he said, good-naturedly shouldering the girls aside. He opened the oven and Alex helped him slide out the huge tin, now filled with a beautiful-looking fruit cake.

"Hm, looks about right," said Toby noncommitally.

"Here — shove this in it," said Roberta Isgrove, holding out a skewer. "See if it's done."

"You prod my cake with that thing, I'll prod you with it," shuddered Toby.

"Well, how do you know it's done then?" asked Jean Taylor.

Toby sighed. "I know," he said. He turned to Miss Talbot. "Can I leave it here until it's cooled off, Delia?" he asked.

"Don't call me Delia," said Miss Talbot automatically, trying to be serious, but in fact the whole school called her Delia after the television cook. She touched the top of the cake lightly. "Yes, of course you can, Toby."

"Good, only can you keep your eye on it? Or

45

these animals will all go breaking pieces off." Anywhere else in the school and Toby would have been set upon but he was in his kingdom in the home economics room. "C'mon then, Alex, I've had a hard morning. You can buy me a soda."

"Yeah, you really worked up a sweat reading that book," said Alex. "Anyway, it's your turn."

The bell for break had just rung and Toby and Alex pushed their way through the churning masses in the corridor. Toby was whistling contentedly to himself when suddenly he broke off. "Oh, good news," he said, "that's *just* what I needed."

Alex looked up to see Maxie Pearson coming down the corridor toward them. He stopped right in front of Alex, blocking his way.

"Well, look who it is," said Maxie. "Christopher Dean — or is it Jane Torvill?"

"Now, if only I'd known you'd be here I'd have brought you a signed photograph," said Alex.

Maxie blinked. "It's Valentine's Day in a couple of weeks and I thought I'd make a card for you to send to your, er, girlfriend." He offered Alex a square of cardboard with a clumsily drawn heart on the front. Alex opened it and Toby craned forward to see what it said:

Roses are Red,
Violets are Blue,

Who is it you perform with?
Now we are through.

Toby winced, expecting that Maxie would soon be receiving the card back internally. Alex had gone white, which was the signal for everyone to duck for cover. But after a couple of fraught seconds he managed to bring himself back under control.

"That's very thoughtful, Maxie," said Alex. "I really had no idea you could read, let alone write." He stepped around Maxie and walked away up the corridor.

"What happened to you, Barnes?" Maxie called after him. "She take all your guts along with her?" Alex didn't answer. Toby made as if to follow after him but Maxie grabbed his jacket.

"You're bending the wardrobe," said Toby, examining Maxie's hand.

"What's wrong with your yellow friend?" Maxie demanded. "I thought he was supposed to be useful?"

"You should know — he stopped your clock back in the sixth grade!"

"We were kids then," said Maxie. "That's why he quit the hockey team — lost his bottle."

"He's just a bit preoccupied at the moment," said Toby. "The day you really get on his nerves the roof's going to fall in."

"I'm terrified."

"Good, you should be." Toby removed Maxie's hand. "Now, if you don't mind, it's ten thirty and I haven't had my elevenses yet."

"You get in the way and I'll be happy to give you a smack, too," offered Maxie.

Toby watched him stride aggressively away in the opposite direction to Alex. "Give me a smack?" said Toby wonderingly. He shook his head in disbelief. "I'm a chef, not a boxer!"

At ten o'clock that night Samantha came creeping down the corridor that led to the gymnasium. This side of the school was deserted at night but even so she was very wary, tiptoeing along in her socks.

Samantha had been sent to bed at six o'clock, as though she were a naughty girl. Mrs. Rollinson had gone up the wall about Samantha dodging her parents but Samantha had just put on her blank expression and had stood there studying the curtains until she had finished. She had been hiding in the linen cupboard, sitting on one of the top shelves behind a pile of towels while they searched the school for her.

She reached the door for the gym, put the light on and stepped inside. There was no chance of the lights being seen because the gym was also used as the theater and had blinds on all the windows.

Samantha had been working on their routines most nights but tonight she didn't feel like going straight into their free dance, so after she had stretched she put on a slow record and started dancing to it, half ballet, half modern. Samantha always expressed emotion with her dancing and she began to feel the music with her body until the dance finally came alive. The record was slow, so was the dance. She let the music play through her, dancing long dramatic movements, as she became one with the record. At last the music faded, leaving her alone in the middle of the gym floor, tears pouring down her face.

Samantha was extremely unhappy! She felt so lonely it was almost a physical pain. She had so wanted to see her parents that morning but wouldn't give in to them. She missed them every day: the brisk no nonsense affection from her mother, and the more protective love of her father. She missed her friends at school, her skating class, and most of all she missed Alex: the friendly training lessons, the half arguments, the occasional explosions, the protests at the morning runs she forced him to take. All she had left were the two ninety-minute skating sessions, which had to be devoted almost exclusively to training.

She sank down on to the floor hugging her knees and let herself cry, really indulging herself in her misery.

"Good evening," said a voice. She jumped. Paula Wallace, one of the prefects, was leaning against the door. Samantha immediately stopped crying and deliberately swore out loud. Paula seemed to find this amusing.

"Oh, it's the Gestapo," said Samantha. "Come on, get it over with — drag me off to Adolph. I'm sure she'll be delighted to see me again today."

Paula came over and, to Samantha's surprise, sat down on the floor beside her. "Why were you crying?" she asked quietly.

"I wasn't! My brain was leaking, that's all."

"If you tell me, it won't go any further."

Samantha sighed. "I'm crying because I'm so happy — all right? Now are you going to turn me in? I should tell you straight, you don't have a lot of choice. I'm already in detention every night for the next ten years as it is, and if you give me lines I won't do them."

Paula smiled. "I'm not going to turn you in," she said. "You don't like it much here then?"

"Oh, I love it."

"Is it your boyfriend, or just the skating?"

"He's not my boyfriend! He's my skating partner," Samantha snapped. "Anyway, how do you know about him?"

"Be serious, everybody knows about you."

"Oh," Samantha said in a small voice.

"You're the most exciting thing here since Denise Maddon ran off with the milkboy," said Paula.

"As long as I manage to keep you all amused," said Samantha.

Paula smiled again. She had a warm smile a bit like Samantha's mother's. A smile much older than Paula's eighteen years.

"You want to give us a chance," she said. "This is a very good school. You'd probably quite enjoy it if you stopped trying to fight the whole world."

"I could never enjoy it here."

"Why not? Most of the other girls do."

"I couldn't — it hasn't got an ice rink."

"Oh, yes — of course."

There was a silence for a moment then Samantha said defensively, "Look, I'm not running your school down, or the other girls — and I'm sure Mrs. Rollinson's OK, but I'm not going to be here long."

"No?"

"No! I'm just here till my father gets over his mega-sulk, then I can go back to my real life."

"I'll be sorry to see you go."

"Oh." Samantha digested this for a moment. "Why?"

"Because that dance you just did was one of the most beautiful things I've ever seen." Paula tilted Samantha's chin up. "My, my, the tough girl can blush then?"

Samantha brushed her arm away and stood up. Paula stood up with her.

"I wanted to be a dancer," Paula said. "My parents wouldn't let me. They sent me here instead." She gave Samantha the benefit of her smile again. "They were right, of course, I couldn't have taken all that work."

"Oh. Look, er, thanks Paula," said Samantha uncertainly.

"That's all right," said Paula. "Don't get caught going back, will you? Or we'll both be in trouble."

8.
Skating on
Thin Ice

Alex and Sue skirted the end of the main rink at the Coliseum and he brought them to a halt in an unprofessional shower of ice.

"You've gotten good," she gasped.

"You have to when you've got Samantha for a partner," said Alex. He glanced at his watch. "We've got time for another run-through before she gets here."

"Forget it, Alex, I want something left for my lesson," she said, still out of breath. "Whatever happened to the laid-back Alex I used to know?"

"He turned serious."

"Are you still going for early morning runs on a weekend?"

"Something to do, you know how it is."

"Yeah, I know," she grinned. "Oh, thank heavens for that, she's here. I'd better go and find my coach." Sue skated off and after a brief word with Samantha disappeared onto the other rink.

"Hi," said Samantha skating up. She wasn't looking happy.

"Hello," said Alex. "You OK?"

She shrugged, "So, so," she said. "Come on, let's not waste any time."

They started running through the inter-silver dances. For the first few minutes they took it easy, giving Samantha time to get warmed up, but then they really threw themselves into it, skating the dances again and again until the sweat was pouring off them. Alex was fit. He had to be as a serious skating competitor, but it was like nothing compared to Samantha. Ten years of classical dance training had forged her slight body out of whipcord. That morning she didn't let up once, no stopping to talk or mess around, just the remorseless grind of the dance.

Alex wasn't about to admit he was exhausted but he was thankful when the one and a half hours had passed.

"It's about time," he said bringing them to a halt.

"We can squeeze one more in," she said, dragging at his arm.

"Hey, hang on," he stopped her.

"What is it? Come on, Alex."

"We haven't even had time to speak yet this morning."

"We're not here to talk."

"Samantha, that's it for the day. We've done

enough," said Alex, deliberately stepping off the ice. She regarded him with disapproval.

"Well, you won't mind if I go around a couple more times," she said.

"Yes, I will!" He reached for her hand and pulled her down onto one of the side benches. "What's up?" he asked.

"Nothing!" She bent down and unlaced her skates. When she looked up again he was still gazing at her.

"I said what's up?" he repeated. "We might be going for a competition, but I used to enjoy my skating."

She sighed. "It's the time, Alex. Three hours a week! We've got so much to fit in."

"Well, it's only temporary, isn't it?" he said. "Look, why don't we forget about the competition and concentrate on the inter-silver?"

"No!"

"I don't want to either but we need the two morning sessions just to practice the medal dances. When are we going to concentrate on the free?"

She was silent for a moment. "I want to enter, Alex."

"All right, how about this? We stick to the same free dance."

"No!"

He picked up her skates and put them away in his bag. Then he said very casually, "This new free dance, have you actually put it together yet?"

"I'm working on it."

"I thought you hadn't."

"Alex, I said I'm working on it," she snapped. "That's the deal, isn't it? You help me with my skating, I'll look after the dancing."

"It's my neck as well if it all goes out the window at the competition!"

"I haven't let you down yet, have I?" she demanded.

"I didn't mean — "

"Didn't you?" she interrupted him, and to his surprise her voice rose to a shout. "I said I'd do it, right? It's my job!" The whole rink was stopping to look at the sound of raised voices.

"Hey, what is all this?" Alex demanded.

"Nothing!" She turned her back on him. After a minute he put his hands on her shoulders from behind. She was shaking.

"You crying?"

"Go away!"

He tried to turn her to face him. She resisted at first, then he managed it and put his arms right around her. After a minute he said quietly: "Bad at school, isn't it?"

She nodded. "It's just me against the whole world," she said.

"There's me."

"But you're not there, Alex." She nearly started to cry again but managed to stop herself at the last moment. They stood there not speaking for a minute then she pulled away.

"I've been thinking," she said, avoiding his eyes.

"Oh, no," he muttered.

"No, seriously," she said. "All this, it's not fair on you. I think you should look around for another partner."

"What?"

"You've got to, Alex," she said. "You can't go through all this every time you want to train. I don't mean Diane. You know there's always girls looking for partners." She kept her eyes firmly fixed on the floor between them. "I'll be all right. I'll be skating seriously again in a couple of years' time and I'll pick up another partner then."

She risked a glance at his face and flinched at his expression. He stared at her for a long moment then suddenly he grabbed her by the shoulders and shook her hard.

"That's the very last time you talk like that!" he said, very angry.

"But I — "

"No, I mean it!" he stormed. "All the trouble I've been to these past weeks: the lies, the creeping around — even poor old Toby doing my paper route! Then I get handed this garbage!" He ran his fingers through his already unruly hair. "Now you listen, Samantha, together we can get through this. But if you decide it's all too much, or if you decide you want another partner, then I won't ever dance again — I'll go back to hockey."

"Oh," she said in a small voice. "Look, Alex — "

"No! I don't want to hear," he said. "Go on, push off before you get me really angry. If you bother to turn up next week you'd better be in a better mood!" He turned away, picked up his sports bag, and disappeared up the corridor, making his exit as dramatic as possible.

Alex glared at the clock in the locker room and made a face. He didn't even have time for a shower. He hurried into his tracksuit, grabbed his bag and stepped outside, and Samantha was waiting. Without a word she slipped her arms around his neck and gave him a kiss. It was a long kiss, the best kiss they'd ever had. Then at last she released him and ran away up the corridor.

Samantha was in a better mood for the rest of the day. Even a furious argument with the math teacher over her homework failed to disconcert her.

Later, that same evening, Paula Wallace came swinging down the corridor whistling to herself. Most of the girls in the high school had their own rooms at Stoke Dameral, though a number of them preferred to share one of the larger bedrooms. She stopped outside one door and knocked on it.

"Back off!" came a voice. A delighted grin broke out on Paula's face. She opened the door and stepped inside. Samantha was sitting on her bed glaring up at her. When she saw who it was, her expression relaxed slightly. "Oh — I thought it was Hitler!" Then, at Paula's puzzled look, she went on, "You know, Hitler? The Principal — inspecting one of her concentration camps."

This delighted Paula even more. "Fortunately for her blood pressure, no," she said. "May I come in?"

"You're in, aren't you?"

Paula went and sat on the end of the bed. "What are you doing?"

"Drawing," said Samantha. Paula picked up Samantha's sketch pad and studied it, a puzzled look on her face. The page was covered with lots of arrows and numbers.

"I'm not into abstract art," said Paula.

"It's a dance," said Samantha.

"Oh — ice skating?"

"Yeah," Samantha admitted. "I've been trying to put a free dance together, but it's not working."

"What's wrong with it?"

"Oh, the moves are all right, but I need a theme," said Samantha. "Something a bit modern, a bit original." She lay back on the bed. "It'll come."

"Mm," ruminated Paula. "So, are you going down to the gym tonight?"

"Me?" Samantha demanded. "You must be joking. I'm grounded for life! I've been a naughty girl, not doing my homework. I have to be in bed by seven. I'm not even supposed to have the light on."

"Ah, it's not that bad."

"I'll tell you the truth," said Samantha. "It's the best part of the day. I can get some work done in peace."

"And you creep downstairs about ten o'clock, do you?"

"Depends," said Samantha.

"What on?"

"Who I'm talking to."

"How d'you mean?"

"You! Are you here as another one of the inmates, or a member of the Gestapo?"

"Did I give you away the other night?"

"No," said Samantha. "I'm still trying to work out why."

"I didn't think it would serve any useful purpose," said Paula. "How many nights do you train then — two?" Samantha shrugged and Paula tried again, "Three . . . four?"

"Seven," Samantha admitted.

"Seven?" Paula said, taken aback. "Why on earth seven?"

"Because there aren't eight days in the week," supplied Samantha.

"Hm — I really should report you, you know."

"Yeah, you should," said Samantha. Then she grinned, the expression only her friends ever saw. "But you're not going to, are you?"

Paula skimmed the sketch pad across the bed. "You're sure your health isn't suffering?"

"Of course not!" Samantha said crossly. "That's just my soft father. He's tried to wrap me in cotton wool ever since I was born. He got worse a couple of years ago when I got rheumatic fever quite badly — now he treats me like an invalid."

"You were ill just before you came here though, weren't you?" said Paula gently.

"Who told you that?" Samantha demanded, sitting up.

"I heard, that's all," said Paula.

"It was just a touch of flu," said Samantha. Then more honestly, "All right, maybe I'm a little more sensitive to colds and stuff like that. They affect my chest. But if I watch it, I'm fine."

There was the sound of footsteps in the corridor outside and the two girls froze, listening to them. Samantha relaxed as they went past the door. She eyed Paula speculatively.

"Paula, what are you doing here anyway? You're not on duty, are you?"

"No, I was just wandering about," said Paula. "Well, actually that's not completely true. The only wondering I was doing was whether you'd mind if I came and watched you dance at night?"

"If you want — why?"

"I thought you might teach me a bit. You know I said I once wanted to be a dancer?"

"You're too old," said Samantha bluntly. "Even for jazz, it's too old to start from scratch."

"I know that," said Paula. "I don't mean serious dance. Just something I could show off at parties."

"Oh, that's different," said Samantha. "Of course I'll help you. In fact we can help one another. I need a partner to make this dance work properly."

"There is a condition though."

"Here we go," sighed Samantha. "I'm not going to behave."

"Oh, no, I know that," said Paula. "It's just that I want you to let me take your temperature each night before we start, and if it's high, you go back to bed."

"You're worse than my dad," said Samantha. "Oh, I suppose, if it'll keep you happy."

"Fine. Come on then, it's nearly eight," said Paula standing up. "Let's get down to the television room."

"What do you mean?"

"Kelly Timpson just had a parcel from her parents."

"Translate that for me, will you?" said Samantha.

"Oh, yes, of course — you wouldn't know," said Paula. "Kelly's father is the British Ambassador in Washington. He sends her all the very latest films on videotape — we sometimes get them here before the cinemas do."

"I can't, I'm grounded — remember?"

"You'll be all right with me," said Paula. She held the door open. Samantha lay staring up at her for a long minute and at last swung her legs onto the floor.

"It'll help pass the time, I suppose," she said offhandedly.

"Wow, so enthusiastic!" grinned Paula. "And careful now, when we get to the television room don't go acting normally. You don't want to go getting accepted by the other girls."

9.
Cloak
and Dagger

It was Wednesday lunchtime, a week later, and Alex had accompanied Toby into the home economics room. Toby was battling with a huge yellow lump of marzipan while Alex helped him by sitting on a desk eating raisins.

"I thought marzipan came in little packets," said Alex idly. Toby turned a horrified gaze on him and shook his head sadly.

"Peasant," he muttered.

"Well, the way you're doing it you'll be here till Christmas." Toby didn't answer, just went on bashing away at the mass with his personal rolling pin.

"Don't go wearing yourself out for tomorrow morning," said Alex. "You're doing my paper route again — remember?"

Toby grunted. "I can hardly wait," he said. "Tell me, have you ever thought of getting a new bike — one that's got brakes?"

"Oh, sure. My dad's just rolling in money — will you ask him, or me?"

"It was just a suggestion," said Toby. "I take it Sam is going to get all this sorted soon? I'm sure all this cycling is bad for my digestion."

"It's good for your figure," said Alex. He sighed. "Look Toby, I really ought to split the money with you."

"Yes, you ought," said Toby, rolling the marzipan into a large square. "Tell me, how are you managing the rink fees lately?"

"I'm skipping lunch and using my dinner money."

"Well, then," said Toby.

"It's still not fair, Toby."

"Just as long as you pay me back when you're famous," said Toby. "Now shut up for a sec, this is the tricky bit."

Carefully he rolled the marzipan halfway around the rolling pin and draped it over the cake, which he had already spread with apricot jam. Then, tongue sticking out in concentration, he eased it down over the corners with the care of an expert covering a billiard table. At last he stood up and gave a sigh of satisfaction: The marzipan was flat and square and there wasn't a wrinkle in sight.

"What are you going to do about Maxie?" asked Toby as he trimmed along the bottom of the cake with a paring knife.

"Eh? How did we get on to Maxie?"

"It's the color of the marzipan, looks gross!" said Toby. "Maxie has the same effect."

"Oh, forget Maxie!"

"I thought you'd have punched his lights out before this, the way he's been carrying on."

"Nobody takes any notice of Maxie."

"Not usually, no, but they do take notice when they see him pushing you around and you just taking it!" said Toby. "I don't get it, what's happened to you?"

"Nothing. I just don't have time to go around fighting everybody anymore."

"You're sure he's not right? About you losing your guts?"

Toby glanced up at his friend's furious face. Toby wasn't worried — there was no way Alex would ever hit him. At last Alex brought himself back under control.

"You don't believe that?" he asked quietly.

"Of course I don't," said Toby. "But I'm about the only one who doesn't."

He disappeared into the pantry and returned with an open packet of store-bought marzipan. He broke Alex off a piece then handed him some of the marzipan he had trimmed off the cake.

Toby watched Alex's face as he chewed. "Now d'you see that for some things it's worth making the extra effort?" he said.

*   *   *

Alex brought them to a halt and gazed at Samantha.

"What happened? Win a swim meet?" he demanded.

"What do you mean?" she asked, surprised.

"It's a bit of a change from last week," he said. "You were actually singing a minute ago."

"It's a lovely day, that's all."

"It's not at all — it's pouring," said Alex. "I hate to think what Toby's going to say. He can't stand getting wet. He gave up swimming in the fifth grade." Samantha wasn't really listening to Alex. She was humming to herself again.

"Let's try that bit of the free again," she said. They went around the ice but halfway through Samantha stopped trying and, letting go of Alex, she drifted away.

"What the — ?" he demanded, but she was going over their last few steps again. "Samantha?" he called.

"Oh, sorry, I just had an idea," she said. "Look, do you think you could do that slow turn again? Only holding me under the arms?"

"You mean like I'm swinging you around?"

"A bit, yeah."

"I should think so," he said. "Let's give it a try." They had a few goes at the turn, finding it reasonably easy.

"Piece of cake," he said. "It's a bit like we did in *Apache*."

"That's the idea! I've tried to keep to the same kind of format so there's not so much to learn," she said. "The only thing is, can you keep hold of me?"

"Well, I just did, didn't I?"

"Mm, but I wanted you to do it for the whole length of the ice."

"No way! You're not that light, kid!"

"And remember you've got to swing me about from side to side as we go."

"You're not listening. I said no!"

"I know, it's a failing of mine." She gave him her sweet smile, which he knew not to trust.

"I take it this is for our new free dance?"

"Mm, well, yes and no. I'm just playing with ideas."

"You're just lying your head off!" he said severely. "You're still set on entering the Juniors?"

"Alex, we have to."

"I don't see it," he said. "Sure, I'd like to enter, but why is this one so important?"

"Because it's the show-piece competition, and Carla Jeffrey and Wayne Jennings are too old to enter this year."

"So what?"

"So everyone's looking for the new Junior stars," she said. "You know how it is with ice dancing. You have to serve your time. Get known, before the judges really start to notice you."

"You're saying that you think we can win it?"

"I think we have to!" Samantha stood looking at him for a long moment, then, "Look Alex, we've won nothing since the Maria Aitkiss competition over a year ago! If we're going to go on up, second and third places are no longer good enough."

"I hadn't even thought of first," he said, nervously running agitated fingers through his hair. Samantha sighed in exasperation. It always took Alex time to believe in himself.

"OK," she said. "When things are going really right, when we're really skating well — you name another couple who can beat us."

"Well, there's Jenny Lynn and Simon Wingate for a start. And then there's — "

"Shut up," she stopped him. "No one's listening Alex. There's just me here, Samantha! Now be honest, you name a couple who can beat us now that Carla and Wayne are no longer in the running."

He shook his head. "Maybe you're right, but it's got to go really well for us and it's not going to do that on two practice sessions a week."

"I'm working on that," she said. "Look, it's getting late. We'd better call it a day."

They skated to the sidelines, Alex still with a worried look on his face. After a second, he asked, "This free dance, it's coming along OK?"

"It's doing all right. I don't want to talk about it for a bit or it'll be jinxed." She sat down on the bench to unlace her skates and deliberately changed the subject. "Say Alex, have you seen that film yet — oh, what's it called again? That guy with the cape?"

"You mean *Cloak and Dagger?*"

"That's the one."

"I went with Toby last week," said Alex. "How come you've seen it? I didn't think they let you out."

"Oh, one of the girls had a pirate video," said Samantha. "What did you think of it?"

"Well, actually I thought it was brilliant," said Alex. "To tell you the truth I didn't like it at all but it's the best film I've seen in years."

"Yes, I thought it was OK," she said.

"I didn't think you watched anything but dance programs?"

"Yeah, I can't exactly choose back at Colditz. What you get is what you get," she said. "Do you think you could do me a favor?"

"No," he said immediately.

She grinned. "It's nothing bad," she said. "It's just that I think the *Cloak and Dagger* theme music is good and I can't get out to buy the record."

"Oh, sure. I'll get it on Saturday when I'm in town," he said. "It's on the charts, isn't it?"

"Is it? I dunno, I just thought it sounded good."
She put her skates away and handed him the bag.
"I'll be off then," she said. Then she stood on tip-
toe and kissed his cheek.

"I think I preferred it when we were arguing,"
he said.

"Eh? What are you talking about?"

"Well, at least I got a proper kiss then," he said.
She smiled at him and this time the kiss was better.

"Tuesday then?" he said after a minute.

"I'll look forward to it," she said to his surprise.
"That swinging turn idea, maybe if you did a few
more push-ups each day — you might have a
think about it. It's quite important." And Alex,
fed up with being pushed around, thought, "She's
not going to *make* me do anything this time." He
turned around to tell Samantha just how he felt,
but she had already disappeared.

10.
Free Dance

It was Saturday morning and that meant compulsory sports practice at Stoke Dameral. From the youngest fifth grader to the Head Girl herself, Mary Boswell, the whole school was required to take part in at least one of the many sports offered. Some of the girls were on a cross-country run. Others had just gone a hundred meters up the road and were pretending they were on a cross-country run. The hockey team, led by Marella, was having a furious battle down on the playing fields, while the less enthusiastic sportswomen were playing a leisurely game of table tennis in the gym.

Paula Wallace was in a hurry. She was late for a tennis game with three of the other prefects. She had been down to the local village and the bus had taken it upon itself to leave half an hour before schedule. Hurriedly Paula flung her tennis clothes on, picked up her racket, and made for the door. At the last moment a faint suspicion stopped her and she skidded to a halt and took a peek into the shower room. She heaved a sigh.

"Samantha, do you have to break every rule in this place?" Paula demanded of the figure who was lying on a bench staring into space.

"Oh, hi, Paula," said Samantha sitting up. "Did you get it?"

"Yes, you'll get me shot!" Paula felt in her sports bag and handed Samantha the latest copy of *Dancing Times*. Samantha grabbed it eagerly.

"Great, thanks, Paula." Samantha had her head buried in it already.

Paula regarded her for a moment, "I suppose it's no good ordering you outside in the sunshine?" she said.

"Waste of breath," said Samantha. Paula grinned, picked up her racket, and dashed off to her game. The morning flew by for all the girls, but especially for Samantha now that she had her magazine to read. She didn't even look up once until the hockey team came thumping noisily into the room close on lunchtime.

"Oh, look who's here," said Marella. "Sportswoman of the year."

Samantha looked up. "Have a nice game did we children?"

"It'd kill you just to get up off your butt!" said Marella.

"That's right, Marella, now run along and play with your dollies." Marella came and stood threateningly over the much smaller Samantha. "I've told you once. We don't want your kind here," she sneered.

"Fine. Do me a favor then. Tell that to the Principal. She might listen — even to you."

The conversation was looking more and more like it was about to turn physical when Mary Boswell put her head around the door.

"What's going on here?" she demanded, scenting the tension in the air. "Marella, what are you doing?"

"She was just asking for my autograph," said Samantha. Marella swore at her.

"Now that's enough!" said Mary crossly. "Marella, I'll pretend I didn't hear that — Samantha, you're wanted by Mrs. Rollinson, right away."

"Oooh, more fun," said Samantha.

"I hope she expels you!" said Marella.

"So do I," said Samantha seriously.

Mrs. Rollinson had her Principal look on again.

"I've a letter here — from your mother," she said.

"Oh, yes."

"She says that you still haven't written a single word to her!"

"I've really nothing to tell her."

"What have you been doing with the stamps I gave you?"

"I stuck them in my stamp album," said Samantha. "It's a hobby I've just taken up. You know, during that riveting hobby hour we get on Sunday nights."

"Don't be impertinent!"

Samantha sighed. Mrs. Rollinson studied her sternly for a moment, then she relaxed, realizing it was all an act. Severity wasn't the answer with this girl.

"Samantha, your parents are worried about you," she said more reasonably.

"They know what they can do then," said Samantha. "I'm more than willing to go home — save a stamp that way."

"Well, I'll tell you what you can do. You can call them up right now — put their minds at rest."

"I get a few dollars a week allowance. I can't afford luxuries like phone calls."

"You may use this one." Mrs. Rollinson pushed her phone across the desk. Samantha regarded it for a moment, then sat down and picked up the receiver. She gazed at it, held it to her ear, then put it down again. "Now what's wrong?"

"I can't with you listening."

"Oh, very well. You can have ten minutes." The Principal rose to her feet and swept from the room.

Samantha smiled to herself, pulled the rolled up copy of *Dancing Times* out of her blazer pocket and turned to the back page. She found the num-

75

ber she wanted and dialed. After a moment it was answered.

"London School of Ballet," said the voice at the other end.

"Er — look, I'm sorry to bother you but is it possible to speak to Abigail Rowe?"

"I'll see if I can find her. Hold please," said the voice. Samantha sat there, seemingly for ages, praying Mrs. Rollinson wouldn't come back. Then at last, "Hello?" said a voice.

"Abby? It's Sam — Samantha Stephens."

"Sammy? It must be a year since I heard from you!"

"Longer than that," said Samantha. "It's nearly eighteen months since I left dance school and it hasn't been easy."

"It never is," said Abigail. "How did you know I was here?"

"I read you'd won a scholarship in this month's *Dancing Times*," said Samantha. "Congrats, that's what you always wanted, wasn't it?"

"I'm not so sure now. I've only been here a month and they've half killed me already," said Abigail. "I heard you'd switched to ice dance — what's it like?"

"A whole new ball game! It's like — oh, I dunno — finally finding your way home," said Samantha. "Look, Abby, I can't talk long, I'm using someone's phone and they'll be back in a sec — I need a favor."

"As long as it's not money," said Abigail.

"I know the feeling," said Samantha. "No, it's not money. Do you still do those Saturday afternoon matinées there?"

"Oh, yeah. I'm dancing in one next month," said Abigail. "Do you want a ticket?"

"Not me, a friend," said Samantha. "I need one of those complimentary season tickets, you know, the ones for friends and family?"

"Oh, I can get you one of those, easy! There's hardly anybody at matinées anyway," said Abigail. "Shall I mail it?"

"No!" said Samantha, hastily. "Can you leave it at the box office to be picked up in my name?"

"I can't manage it for today. It's not long before they open."

"Next week'll be fine."

"Consider it done then."

"Thanks a million, Abby. You've saved my life," said Samantha.

"Yes, but how?"

"I'll write and explain," said Samantha. "I've got plenty of stamps. I'll have to go, she's coming back — best of luck next month." Samantha got the phone back down just as Mrs. Rollinson opened the door.

"Did you get through?" the Principal asked in a much more friendly tone.

"Yes, thank you."

"Ah — see, it's not that hard really, is it? If you talk things through, you can sort any problem out."

"Yes, Mrs. Rollinson," said Samantha standing up. "I'm learning that."

11.
Floor Show

It was thirty minutes by bus to the Coliseum. Samantha leaned against the window in one of the rear seats, still only half awake. The number of girls going swimming went up and down, like a barometer with the weather, which made it easier for her to escape notice. Even so, she kept a low profile. Today, for the first time, she could hear Marella's strident voice from the front of the bus.

The bus stopped right outside the main doors and they all piled out and into the locker room. Samantha put on her black leotard, the one that looked exactly like a bathing suit. Then she deliberately hung around waiting for the others to disappear to the various swimming pools.

"Oh, look, her Highness has graced us with her presence," said Marella, noticing Samantha for the first time. "I thought you didn't like sports?"

"This is exercise, not a game," said Samantha. "Though I'm very glad to see you here, Marella."

"Sure you are!"

"No, seriously," said Samantha. "It was well time you got around to having a bath."

Marella's face froze. She glared around, but Mrs. Clarke, the sports teacher, was still rounding up her beginners' class. Marella turned back to Samantha.

"One of these days there won't be anybody around to protect you," she snapped.

"Wow, I'm *really* worried," Samantha said.

Marella grabbed up her towel and banged away through the changing-room doors. Samantha waited until Mrs. Clarke had escorted the last of her girls towards the beginners' pool before she donned her tracksuit and slid out of the other door, the one that led to the rink.

Alex was waiting, looking a little impatient. Samantha was feeling affectionate and she wanted to give him a hug but she could tell it wasn't the right time.

"Oh, you're here?" he said.

"Evidently," she said quietly.

"Well, we'd better get started, hadn't we?"

"Good idea — is it all right if I put my skates on first?" she said.

"Get a move on!" He stood sighing while she laced up her skates, then took her hand and almost dragged her out onto the ice. Routinely they went straight into the dances for their medal test. Their only dialogue was about the skating and gradually even this desultory conversation faded. Finally Samantha stopped watching where she was going and instead she fixed her eyes on his face. After a minute or so he felt her gaze, met her eyes, and they let their skating slow to a halt.

"Are you going to tell me what's wrong?" she said.

"Nothing," he said.

"Oh, yeah, sure there isn't!" she said. She was silent for a moment, then, "You know, Alex, I look forward to Tuesdays and Thursdays all week. They're the only thing that keep me going. Are you trying to ruin that for me as well?"

"You mean you look forward to the skating?"

"You know what I mean."

"Yes, of course," he said, an ashamed look on his face. He put his arms right around her. "I'm sorry, Samantha, I've just had a bad week. I got a bit fed up when you were late and took it out on you."

"I can live with that — that's what partners are for," she said. "But don't shut me out, eh?"

"Sorry," he said. "After all, you're never moody, are you?"

"What me?" she said, wide-eyed with innocence.

"I was late because I've got to be extra careful for a bit — there's a girl here this morning who would just love to catch me skating."

"Oh! Do you want to cut the session short?"

"I don't! It'll be all right if I watch my step. This place is as big as a town, the swimming pools are miles away, and they're usually packed," she said. "Most of the girls don't even think about there being skating rinks here — I'm sure Hitler doesn't even know they exist or she wouldn't let me near."

"OK." He pushed her backwards so he could look at her. "So how was your week?"

"Terrific," she said. "What was wrong with yours?"

"Maxie's being a jerk."

"Is that all?"

"It's not just him. It's all the others following his lead," said Alex. "You wouldn't understand. That sort of thing doesn't happen in girls' schools."

"No!" she said wryly, but Alex wasn't sensitive enough to notice.

"Never mind, let's forget it," he said. "Let's see what you've come up with for our free."

"OK, I'll take you through a few bits of it."

"And I've got to skate in a cloak, have I?"

She stared at him in surprise. "I'm sorry," she said after a moment.

"What for?"

"Taking you for an idiot."

He grinned. "I've got the music for you," he said. "I've even taped it for our Walkmans."

"Thanks, Alex."

"You do realize of course, how it's got to start and finish?"

"Yes, I do realize that," she said sarcastically.

"And, consequently, how big the cloak has got to be? It's going to be difficult not to get it caught up," he said.

"If it was easy everybody would be doing it," she said. "Oh, Alex, you'll manage it."

"I'm glad you've got confidence in me," he said.

"Of course I've got confidence in you!" she said seriously. "All you've got to do is practice enough so it becomes second nature. If you can think of a way of practicing on your own, it'd help."

"I don't know about that," he said. "Anyway, what about you? When are we going to practice together?"

"I thought Saturday afternoons," she said casually. "Three o'clock till six."

"What?" he demanded. "I thought you weren't allowed out without a keeper?"

"Yeah," she grinned. "I'll handle that. I need you to get Liz to give the rink manager here a call. Ask his permission for us to use the small rink, out of the crowds."

"Oh, she'll do that," said Alex. "Well, let's see what you've managed to come up with."

Samantha started taking him through the routine. Suddenly she felt he wasn't concentrating and when she looked up he was laughing.

"What now?" she demanded.

"Oh, nothing, " he said. "Only, are you going to tell Toby, or me?"

"What about?"

"About him doing my Saturday evening paper route as well!"

Alex fixed the sheet to his cuffs with safety pins and studied himself in the changing-room mirror. The sheet flapping around his feet, which sported a bright yellow pair of roller skates, made him look like a demented seagull. Alex was fully aware of how silly he looked and he needed to get to the gym without being noticed. There was a fire escape that led from the locker rooms to the back door of the gym.

The Principal was showing the two new school Professors around the premises. It wasn't his favorite duty but he realized the necessity of making a good impression with this Mrs. Barr and Sir Peter Brooke.

"This is the gymnasium," the Principal was saying. "We take sport very seriously here — " He broke off because neither of the Professors were watching him, their eyes were fixed on the figure of one of his ninth graders wrapped up in a billowing sheet, clanking down the fire escape in roller skates.

Alex decided only a show of nonchalance would carry him through. "Good afternoon," he said. "Lovely day, isn't it?" He strolled as fast as he could past the three frozen figures and ducked around the corner of the gym to safety and right into the middle of the fifth-grade nature club who were out looking for ladybugs. Hordes of little girls seemed to be pointing fingers at him and laughing. Alex struggled proudly through.

"Alex, what are you doing?" demanded Miss Rawlings, the biology teacher.

"Just getting a breath of fresh air, Miss Rawlings," said Alex, ducking through the door into the gym and safety.

"Do you mind?" said an irate Phil Price, hurriedly letting go of Roberta Isgrove. She gave an exasperated sigh.

"Oh, let's go to the corridor at the back of the gym," she repeated sourly. "Nobody ever goes there!"

"Sorry," said Alex. "Don't mind me, I'm just coming through." They watched him in silence as he clumped along the corridor and finally made it into the gymnasium.

"Why d'you think he's dressed like that?" Roberta Isgrove asked.

"I didn't want to ask," said Phil Price. "Oh, never mind — he's never been all there, has he?"

Alex shut the door on the world and stood in the empty gym breathing heavily.

"The things I do for you, Samantha Stephens," he muttered. "I might as well have come down the main corridor — it wouldn't have been as busy!" He examined his feet; the roller skates didn't feel right: not as smooth, not as fast, not as free. And certainly not as safe. He switched on his Walkman and cautiously set off down the length of the gym. The sheet behaved well until he tried to turn, then it wrapped itself spitefully around the wheels of his one skate and he hit the floor with a crash. Alex was well used to hitting the floor, or rather the ice, but the unexpectedness of this fall took his breath away. He picked himself up and tried again.

It happened every single time. If he turned fast the sheet trapped his innermost skate, and if he slowed right down, it was lying in wait for the other one. Still he kept on until the one side of his body felt like a huge bruise. Finally, one of his more spectacular falls dislodged his Walkman and he switched it off, realizing he was in danger of smashing it. So this time, when he hit the floor, he heard cheers.

He looked up, shocked out of his preoccupation. Half the school seemed to be standing outside the windows, all pointing and laughing: The fifth-grade nature club had abandoned their quest for ladybugs and were standing right at the front. Roberta Isgrove and Phil Price had given up romance for laughter and were leaning against each other, almost convulsed. The only good thing was that there was no sign of the Principal or his two visitors.

Alex couldn't stop now or everybody'd know it was because of them. He scrambled up and rolled down the gym, knowing what an idiot he must look with the sheet billowing around him.

"Here he comes — watch now." He could clearly hear Maxie's voice giving the running commentary. "And turn, and . . . crash!" Everybody broke into applause as Alex went down yet again.

"Come on, everybody," shouted Maxie. "This is the latest idea in skating. It's called the Kamikaze quickstep — oh! And that gesture he just made must mean it lasts two minutes."

Alex got slowly to his feet and stood there feeling lonely. He needed Samantha more than ever before, needed her support. Last year when this sort of thing had happened she genuinely hadn't seemed to care. But on his own, Alex cared!

Crossly he wrenched the sheet free, tearing it in his haste and stormed out of the gym. Even then he managed to give them all a final thrill — he forgot he was wearing roller skates and went through the door on his backside.

12.
Soft Ice

"**N**o! No! No! No! No!" Alex cried. "I've told you a hundred times, you can't step back or you'll fall over the cloak."

"Sorry," she said quietly. Alex pushed her unceremoniously around so they faced back down the ice.

"Now this time concentrate!" he rapped. He held his arms out, high up, so they completely circled her head. She stood up very close, her hands flat against his chest, trying to imagine a cloak surrounding her. This time they nearly made it, Alex's one strong push propelling them down the rink, but then two thirds of the way she felt the momentum fade and automatically moved a skate back to keep her balance.

"What is *wrong* with you!" he raged, clutching his hair and turning away in exasperation. "You're not usually this thick!" He took a deep breath to regain his composure, then he turned back to her. "Now listen, Samantha . . ." his voice trailed away because now he looked her in the face, it wasn't Samantha, it was Sue. Sue, who at nineteen was four years older than he, who was only six months away from getting married. Sue, who had been his baby sitter. Sue, who was now standing grinning at him.

"Or, er, sorry, Sue," he muttered. "I got so wrapped up I forgot it was you."

"Don't worry, Alex, I think it's lovely," she said, patting his tousled hair back into place. He stepped back out of range.

"Sorry I went a bit crazy," he said. "That's how we are — Samantha and me."

"Is she any better with this cloak idea than I am?" asked Sue.

"Well, she, er — " he broke off, embarrassed.

"Yes?"

"Well, to be perfectly honest, she trusts me more," he admitted. "Even if she thinks she's about to fall, she'll stay in position. I've dumped her on her head a number of times."

"Sounds terrific! I'm glad I'm an individual skater," said Sue.

"The cloak's still getting in the way though," said Alex. "Especially when we're going backwards. We've tried it with the sheet and it just blows back against your legs and gets all tangled up."

"It needs to be made of a heavier material," said Sue. "And remember, she's a lot smaller than

I am — if anyone can make it work, you two can."

"Heavier," Alex mused. He held his arms out again as though encircling his partner and skated a few thoughtful steps. Sue glanced at her watch.

"Look, Alex, I must get going. I'm meeting Brian."

"Aw, not yet, Sue. You said you were OK till eight."

"Yeah — and it's eight thirty already," said Sue. "He'll be having a fit as it is."

"Oh — right, OK," said Alex. "You'd better go."

"D'you want a lift?"

"No, I'll stay for a while. I've got nothing else to do." He gave her a vague smile and glided away to the middle of the ice. In spite of her hurry Sue stood watching him for a minute, wondering at the transformation that had taken place over the last year. There was no trace of the laid-back, uncaring Alex of old. The boy who would never bother to train.

The rest of the dance class had broken up an hour before and now the outside of the ice was crammed with leisure skaters. The only other real skaters there were Diane and her new partner, Colin. They were running through their free dance for the Juniors.

At ten thirty the PA system announced the ice was to be cleared. After a minute, the announcement was made again, only this time more sternly, and gradually the ice emptied. The rink manager finished switching off all the lights upstairs and trooped down to the rink knowing what he'd find. Sure enough, one lonely figure was still skating around the center of the ice. The rink manager rapped sharply on the windows and the figure gave a start, gazed blankly around the deserted rink, then came hurrying over.

"Sorry, I forgot," said Alex breathlessly.

"That's all right, Alex," the rink manager said. "I've got to get home sometime tonight, you know."

"I'll be right there," he said. "I'll just grab my things." The rink manager watched as Alex dashed into the locker room.

"That's all right," he repeated to himself. "I wouldn't like it to be said one day that we once threw a world champion out."

Carefully Toby squeezed the icing bag and added another delicate line of tracery to the lattice that now covered his cake. It was Monday afternoon's home economics lesson and a line of chairs had been set up barricading Toby off from the rest of the class. The only people allowed on his side were Alex, who was sitting in his usual place on the desk top looking considerably more anxious than Toby did, and Hilary Anderson, a girl from seventh grade who was following in Toby's footsteps.

"Don't throttle the bag, caress it," Toby was saying to Hilary, who was hovering at his elbow. Alex found this funny. Hilary didn't, she nodded respectfully.

"You don't think the icing's a bit soft?" she asked.

"No, it'll set all right," said Toby. "It hasn't got to be that hard as it's not supporting another tier." He glanced up at Alex. "How did Saturday go?" he asked.

"I don't know what you mean," said Alex. "Saturday? What happened on Saturday?"

"Oh, you can talk in front of H," said Toby. "Listen H, keep your mouth shut, will you?"

"Hm, oh sure," said Hilary, not caring. Her gaze was still fixed on Toby's skillful icing.

"It went fine," said Alex. "We managed a whole three hours."

"I thought she had to have a prefect with her when she went out?"

"Yes, but she's made friends with one," said Alex. "And she just happens to be a ballet fan, so Samantha's got her fixed up with a free ticket for a matinée every Saturday."

"Smart! *Very* smart," said Toby.

"Oh, you know what she's like," said Alex.

"You still only seeing her for skating?"

"What does that mean?"

"Well, you're not taking her out?"

93

"How can I?" demanded Alex. "The small amount of time we get together we have to spend skating — oh, it doesn't matter. We'd rather skate than waste time going to see a film or something."

"What about Valentine's night?"

"Eh?"

"We're going to need more icing," said Toby to Hilary. "D'you think you could get started on some?"

"Are you sure?" Hilary asked, worriedly.

"You'll do fine," said Toby. "Just leave the glycerine to me." She went off to the other side of the room and Toby turned his attention back to Alex. "It's Valentine's Day on Friday," he said. *"The* event of the year!"

"Well, you don't seriously think they're going to let Samantha out for the night, do you?" Alex demanded.

"Of course not," said Toby. "But there are other girls around, you know — nobody's taking Bobby Isgrove yet, as far as I know."

"Bobby? She'll be going with Phil Price."

"No she won't! They had one heck of a break up," said Toby.

"Yeah?" said Alex interestedly. "What happened?"

"Well, they were supposed to be going to the Barn dance on Friday night but he said he had too much homework, so they both decided to stay in," said Toby. "Then she caught him taking Jean Taylor instead."

"Was there an argument?"

"You said it! She was with Colin Williams," grinned Toby. "There was quite a fight."

"Between Colin and Phil?"

"No! Between Roberta and Phil, of course," said Toby. "So how about it? She's not fixed up with anybody else yet as far as I know."

"Aw, I don't like it."

"Don't fancy Bobby Isgrove you mean?" said Toby. "Wow, you have got it bad."

"I have not!" said Alex. "I just get enough dancing on the ice."

"Yeah?" There was a silence between them for a minute. "Is *she* going to a dance?"

"I think there's one at the school."

"They're all girls, aren't they?" Toby said, looking up in surprise.

"Oh, they bring in some posh boys' school for dances and plays, that sort of thing," said Alex.

"There you are then," said Toby. "Sammy wouldn't mind — she wouldn't even know."

"I'll see," said Alex.

" 'Course you will."

"Well, who are you going with?" Alex said, changing attack.

Toby gestured with his eyebrows. "H," he said.

"Hilary?" said Alex, aghast. "What, silly Hilary?"

"If you bother to take a close look at her, you'll find she's no longer silly," said Toby coldly. "She's got a lot going for her."

Alex gazed across the room at Hilary, who was working away at a mound of icing. It was true, in the last year Hilary had changed out of all recognition.

"You kept that a bit quiet," said Alex.

Toby grinned. "We've got a lot in common," he said. "She's not much on cakes but her pastry's the best in junior high."

Alex sighed. "You're not normal," he said.

Toby looked up from his icing. "And you are?" he said, letting the question hang in the air.

13.
Ice-Cold
Reception

Samantha was sitting in the corner of the television room, sewing a length of pure silver material. It was seven o'clock on Thursday evening, just after prep, and the room was packed with girls all discussing the Valentine's dance on the following night. Marella was at the center of it. She had brought down armfuls of dresses and everyone was taking turns trying them on.

Marella deliberately came up to Samantha, dressed in an over-the-top number that didn't suit her at all.

"Trying to get that finished for tomorrow night?" she demanded, flicking one of her hanging veils in Samantha's face. Samantha ignored her, just went on sewing. She wasn't very good at needlework but she was taking a lot of care.

"What a shame your boyfriend won't be there," said Marella, probing for Samantha's weakness. Then, when she didn't get a reaction, "Well, I suppose it's for the best. He'd probably feel out of place." Samantha carefully threaded another length of thread through her needle.

"Tell you what," persisted Marella. "You come along tomorrow night and I'll introduce you to some boys who, er, shall we say, don't belong to the proletariat?"

"What's going on here?" said an icy voice. Marella turned and went down like a pricked balloon. Paula was standing in the doorway wearing her best prefect's expression.

"Nothing, Paula," Marella said.

"I wasn't aware that this had been turned into a fitting room," said Paula.

"We were just trying on a few dresses for tomorrow."

"Well, go and put them away," said Paula. "Hurry up." Marella looked mutinous but she strode off to do as she was told. Paula sat down beside Samantha.

"You don't have to fight my battles for me," said Samantha quietly.

"I'm just doing my job, Samantha," said Paula. "Now, what's this nonsense I hear about you not coming tomorrow night?"

"It's not nonsense."

"Don't be so silly. Everybody comes to the Valentine's dance."

"I want to stay in and get this finished," said Samantha. Paula examined the dress on which Samantha was working.

"Hm, expensive bit of material. Silk, isn't it?"

"Yes, it's an old party dress of mine."

"Not so old," said Paula. "Was it for tomorrow night? Is that why you're not coming?"

"No! It's for something more important than a dance," said Samantha.

"So you do have something you could wear?"

Samantha smiled to herself. "I expect I'd manage," she said.

"Well, come then, for me," urged Paula.

Samantha heaved a sigh. "If you say it like that, I've got to," she said. She held up the silver dress. "I suppose I could finish this another night."

"There's not much left to do is there?"

"Not on this, no," said Samantha. "I still need a large piece of heavy material, though."

"Ask Mrs. Mount, the needlework teacher."

"She'll want to know what it's for." Samantha looked up as the school secretary put her head around the door. "Oh no, now what?" she muttered.

"How do you know it's for you?" demanded Paula.

"It's always for me," said Samantha, resigned.

"Samantha Stephens," called the secretary.

"Yes, Mrs. Williams?"

"Mrs. Rollinson's study, right away, please." Then she was gone.

"Oh, Samantha, what have you been up to now?" Paula sighed.

"Nothing," said Samantha getting wearily to her feet. "Well, nothing more than usual, anyway."

Samantha knocked on the familiar door and walked in. She froze. "Sh — " she just stopped herself in time. Her parents were sitting gazing at her. There was no sign of Mrs. Rollinson.

"Is that the kind of language you learn here?" asked her father.

Samantha was about to deny it, but changed her mind. "Yes, Father, all the girls speak like that."

Her mother sighed. "Nice try, Samantha," she said. "Now, have you got a kiss for your mother and father?"

"If that's what you want," Samantha said offhandedly. She gave each of them the briefest kiss she could manage, and sat down away from them.

"We've come to find out why you haven't written to us," said her father. Samantha shrugged and studied the toes of her polished brown shoes.

"Mrs. Rollinson says she has given you any number of stamps," said Mrs. Stephens. "So what have you been doing with them?"

"I've stuck them in an album. I've taken up stamp collecting," said Samantha. "It's all there is to do here at Colditz."

"Oh, Samantha, stop being stupid," said her mother crossly.

"How are you getting along? Made any friends yet?" put in her father.

"No!"

"What about generally? Settling in?" Her father still kept trying.

"I can't do the work," said Samantha. "I'm so far behind the others that I'm out of sight."

"We're well aware of that," said her mother. "Mrs. Rollinson informs us that you won't even try to do the work."

"It's all totally different here," said Samantha. "I can't understand anything."

Her parents studied her for a moment, then her father spoke, "It's not going to work, Samantha," he said. "This attitude only makes me more confident that we did the right thing sending you here. If you refuse to work all that will happen is that you'll be put back a year."

"Why should you care if I work or not?" Samantha suddenly lost her temper. "You've got what you wanted, haven't you? Me out of the way!"

"That's not fair, Samantha," said her father. "You know why you were sent here."

"Anything you say, Father," said Samantha. She glanced at her watch. "Thank you for coming to visit me — I mean on a Thursday, too. I bet you had to miss your golf."

Mr. Stephens' face looked stricken. Without another word he stood up and left the room, shutting the door quietly. Samantha was watching him, her insides twisting, stopping herself running after him. Mrs. Stephens started to follow her husband but stopped at the door and looked back at her daughter.

"Are you satisfied now?" she said.

"I didn't say anything that wasn't true," said Samantha standing up. "He doesn't give a darn about me." Mrs. Stephens stood glaring at her daughter for a long moment, then she brought her hand up and slapped her across the face. Samantha fell back more in shock than pain.

"You have no idea how upset he is about all this," said her mother, angrier than Samantha had ever seen her before. "No idea, Samantha! You're breaking his heart!" When she swept out, *she* slammed the door.

Paula was waiting patiently in the corridor. She watched as an upset Mr. Stephens almost ran away up the corridor followed by the even more dramatic exit of Mrs. Stephens and sighed at the looks on their faces. Paula went quietly into the Principal's study. Samantha was sitting on the floor in a huddle, crying. She sat down beside her and put an arm around her.

"Come on now, Samantha," she said gently. "It can't have been that bad?"

"She hit me," wept Samantha. "My mother hit me!"

"I expect you deserved it," said Paula.

"But my parents have never hit me in my life," said Samantha. She wiped her sleeve across her eyes. "They must really hate me."

"Oh, don't talk such rubbish," said Paula. "If they didn't care, they wouldn't even get upset."

14.
Breaking the Ice

At seven o'clock on Friday the fourteenth of February, excitement was running high at Stoke Dameral. Marella shared one of the larger rooms with Genna. She was sitting studying herself in the dressing-table mirror; she reached for a lipstick and started to apply it carefully.

"I don't know why you're so down on her," said Genna, who was fussing with her hair over Marella's shoulder.

"Ah, she's such a wimp," said Marella. "All this talk about her being a professional athlete."

"She's all right. You just like having someone to pick on."

"Yes, well she'd better not be there tonight, that's all," said Marella.

"Why? She won't affect you."

"No?" Marella eyed her in the mirror. "What about when it comes to the dancing?"

"What d'you mean?"

"Think thickhead!"

"Oh, you mean she's a trained dancer?"

"That's right. She'll make the rest of us look sick," said Marella. "Still, I don't think she's got much to wear. Her parents only give her a couple of dollars a week allowance." Marella fumbled in her drawer and brought out a cut-glass perfume spray, it was nearly empty.

"Darn, I'll have to get some more," she said.

"What? Chanel No. 5?"

"Yes, my mother will buy some for me when she comes down on Founder's Day," said Marella, spraying herself comprehensively.

"What the hell's that?" gasped Genna. "It smells like bad eggs!"

"Aaah! What is it?" cried Marella coming to her feet. She sniffed the spray, then, "It's this darn perfume."

"Ugh!" Genna had backed right away and was holding a handkerchief to her nose. "Has it gone bad?"

"Don't be so stupid, Chanel No. 5 doesn't go bad!" Marella was frantically tearing at her clothes.

"Careful of your dress," said Genna.

"It hardly matters, does it?" demanded Marella. "I can't wear it now! Oh, I'll have to have another shower, wash my hair — everything."

"I don't understand — how'd it happened?"

"Someone's been at it, of course," said Marella. "Oooh, you just wait till I get my hands on them." Genna was struggling with the window — the smell was awful and it filled the room like a cloud. Marella was struggling into her dressing gown. Suddenly she froze.

"Gen," she said in a horrified whisper. "What am I going to wear?"

Samantha timed her entrance to perfection. She waited until the dance had begun and most of the male guests were there. The girls and the visitors were still eyeing one another up. Marella, trying to hide herself behind the soft drinks table, was wearing her summer school dress. Everything else she had was either being laundered or needed ironing, and Marella was too big to borrow from any of the other girls.

Suddenly both the double doors flew open and Samantha was standing there, a demure smile on her face. A hush fell over the room as every eye turned in her direction. She stood there a minute for the full effect, then strolled unself-consciously down the very center of the room. Gradually the conversation picked up again but now everybody kept glancing in her direction. Paula was helping serve the fruit punch, but she abandoned it and went over to Samantha.

"Hi, Paula," said Samantha.

"What are you nearly wearing?" sighed Paula.

"Don't you like it?" Samantha gave a twirl.

Samantha was dressed in a dance costume that was so modern it was outrageous. Made of some silvery material that glittered and flashed in the lights, it was so tight that it clung like a second skin. There was a large hole cut in the front of it revealing a stomach as flat as a board that had every girl in the room hating her.

"Well, I like it," said Paula. "And I'm sure every boy in the room does, but I should steer clear of Mrs. Rollinson if I were you."

"Aah, what can she do?" Samantha tossed her head, really getting into the part.

"She can send you to change," said Paula. Samantha looked around to make sure no one was listening.

"I don't really care if she does, now," she said *sotto voce*. "I was only doing it to put Marella's nose out of joint."

"You've done that all right," said Paula. "Though it's a pity if you go just yet. There's a boy over there who's definitely interested in you." In spite of herself Samantha glanced around to see.

"He's quite good-looking," said Paula.

"Hm," said Samantha. "He's all right, I suppose. Not really my type — can I have some punch?" Paula handed her a glass and she sipped it and made a face.

"I don't suppose you've got any gin?" she said.

"Don't try and be as sophisticated as you look," said Paula. "Where did you get that outfit from, anyway?"

"It's an old dance costume from a production I was in at dance school," said Samantha. "I just had to let it out a bit."

"Pity you couldn't have let it out a bit more," said Paula dryly. "Uh, oh, here he comes!" The boy had finally gathered up his courage and was coming over. Samantha deliberately turned her back, but he wasn't put off.

"Wouldn't you like a dance?" said a voice from behind.

"I don't mind," she said offhandedly. "Someone's got to start them off, I suppose." They went out onto the empty floor. A slow record was playing, so he put his arms around her shoulders and they did a slow swaying dance with everybody watching them.

"Do you come here often?" he said after a minute.

"Now that is original," she said.

"Look, I'm trying," he said. "Er, you're dressed very conservatively."

"This old thing?" said Samantha airily.

"None of the other girls seem to be dressed like that."

"No, well — I'm the Principal's favorite," she said. "She asks to see me virtually every day."

"That's nice," he said. "What did you say your name was?"

"I didn't," she said. "But it's Natalia — Natalia Makarova."

"Natalia? That's Russian isn't it? My name's Mikhail Baryshnikov."

"That's Russian as well, isn't it?" she said. They danced in silence for a few moments then Samantha glanced up at him.

"There's just one thing I want to know?"

"What is it?"

"How did you get *in*, Alex?"

"Walked," he said. "I left my bike in some bushes outside the main gates and just followed the bus in. All the staff think I'm from the other school."

"Are you keeping an eye on me?"

"I need to if you intend to go around dressed like that."

"I'll dress how I like, Alex Barnes!" she said crossly.

"Hey," he gave her shoulders a gentle shake. "I just came to be with you, that's all right, isn't it?"

"Yes, sorry," she said quietly.

"I thought you'd be pleased to see me."

"Of course I am," she said, giving him a small

smile. She sighed, "Alex, I'm dressed like this to show the other girls, that's all. I wasn't going to stay long."

"You're a free agent, Samantha," he said. "You can do what you like."

"I know that," she said quickly. "I wasn't justifying myself. I was just saying, that's all — are you laughing at me?"

"No — of course not," he grinned. Then as the music changed, "Ah, that's better. Let's wake this lot up."

Alex couldn't dance like Samantha, but even so his ice-dance training put him miles ahead of everybody else in the room. And as for Samantha! She'd been dancing since she was four and her whole life was devoted to dance. They stood slightly apart but moved as one person, letting the music play through their bodies, totally lost in the experience. Others found the courage to push out onto the floor but Alex and Samantha were left in their own little space. A unit of brilliance in an average group.

Finally, after a solid half hour that would have left an ordinary person exhausted, they were brought back to earth when the music changed tempo again.

They retreated to the drinks table.

"This end," Samantha whispered. "Steer clear of the staff, will you?" Alex glanced at the other end of the table where the three teachers all had disapproving looks on their faces.

"What's through there?" Alex nodded to the big open French window.

"That's the balcony," said Samantha. "We're allowed to go outside with the boys as long as we stay on the balcony." She grinned and added, "To — er, cool off."

"Wow — daring," said Alex.

"They like to keep an eye on us. Hitler said at assembly that it was in case things got out of hand."

"I should have gone to the school dance," said Alex. "Things always get out of hand there — say, did you know Toby's going out with Hilary Anderson?"

"Oh, good for him," said Samantha. "I didn't think he had the time, what with his cooking and your paper route."

"He's a bit of a downer, our Toby," said Alex.

"She's that pretty girl from seventh grade, isn't she?"

"Yes — I understand he greatly admires her cream puffs," grinned Alex. "He told me she's the best pastry maker in the seventh grade."

Samantha hit him with her elbow. "I'm glad he's got someone to spend time with him," she said. "You're always using him."

"I'm not! He's a friend," said Alex indignantly. "Friends do one another favors."

"Absolutely," said Samantha. "So you can do me a favor if you like."

"I can hardly wait."

"Please, Alex — for me." She leaned forward and whispered in his ear.

He frowned. "But why?" he asked. "I dunno Samantha, it doesn't seem a very nice thing to do!"

"Oh, go on, Alex," she urged. "It's very important to me."

"You mean the girl over there who's been glaring at you all night."

"That's the one."

He sighed. "Well, I'll see," he said. "But it won't have any effect, anyway."

"Trust me," said Samantha. Then she gave him her sweetest smile. "I'll meet you afterwards on the balcony. I'm — er, going to cool off."

He stood there finishing his drink, watching as Samantha disappeared through the glass door. Then making up his mind he put down his glass and went over to where Marella was leaning against the wall.

"Hi," he said, trying to be original.

"Er, hello," said Marella, taken aback. No one had bothered with her yet that evening.

"Would you like a dance?"

"Well, I don't mind," she said, taking the chance

to get back at Samantha. Alex led her out onto the floor, which was now much more packed as things really got under way. The music was fast for two records, then slowed right down, and Alex could put his arms around her. Now they could talk.

"I haven't seen you at one of our dances before," said Marella.

"I haven't been to one," said Alex. "They're not bad — the music's quite good, isn't it?"

"Oh, I think it's awful," said Marella. "In the Christmas holidays I went to Stringfellows — now that's more my kind of scene. They seem to let anybody in here."

"Hm," said Alex, realizing that Samantha wasn't wrong about this girl. He decided that now he could go through with it. "There's a bit of a funny smell in here though, isn't there?" he said.

"I can't smell anything," she said, stiffening in his arms.

"No?" He sniffed the air. "It's a bit like bad eggs."

Marella almost screamed. She pulled away and sniffed at her arms, regarding him in horror. Then she bolted from the room. Alex stood there for a minute, stunned at her reaction. Hurriedly he retreated to the balcony to get away from the mass of staring eyes. Samantha, who had been watching it all, gave him her first real smile of the evening.

"Oh, that was wonderful," she said.

"Yeah? Would you like to explain what it was all about?" he asked.

"Oh, never mind," she said. "It doesn't matter." She linked her hands behind his neck.

"Hey," he said. "I thought you came out here to cool off."

"Alex," she said seriously. "That's the last thing I want to do."

15.
On Velvet

Alex watched as Samantha pulled yard after yard of black material from her sports bag. It was Thursday morning and for once the ice was busy with skaters and their coaches.

"Do you think it's big enough?" he said sarcastically.

"It's exactly the right size," she said. "I sat up most of the night making sure." He picked up the huge cloak.

"Hey, Samantha, this is velvet, isn't it?" he demanded.

"It was the only material I could find heavy enough."

"It must have cost a fortune."

"Nah, I took it — it's cheaper," she said sweetly.

"Took it?" he said aghast. "You can't go around taking great masses of material."

"Our need was greater." She shrugged. "Aw, I wouldn't worry about it if I were you. It was just

115

some old velvet left hanging around — nobody'll miss it." She fitted the collar around his neck. "Now let's see — I think that'll do quite nicely."

He slipped his thumbs through the two loops that kept the cloak in place and stood there looking a bit like a vulture, with the massive cloak spread around him, hanging to just above the floor.

"You've got the length just about perfect," he said.

"Of course — how's the weight?"

"Heavy! Oh, I'll get used to it," he said. "Let's see how it feels on the ice."

They took a couple of turns around the rink, very wary of the heavy cloak, but the weight actually made it more controllable. It didn't flap around like the sheet, but swung slowly, giving the effect they had been after. They stopped at the end of the rink and smiled at each other.

"It's going to work," he said.

"Did you ever doubt me?"

"Not really," he shook his head. "Now all we have to do is fit it to the routine."

"Well, we'll have a full run through on Saturday," she said.

"There's a problem with this Saturday," he said. "I can't make it."

"What? Of course you can make it! You have to make it!"

"I'm sorry, Samantha, I'm out all day."

"Whatever it is, cancel it! After all the trouble I went to get Saturdays together — you cancel it, Alex!"

"One Saturday won't hurt."

"And do you know how many Saturdays we've got left?" she demanded. "Three! That's all. Three!"

"Look, Sue's skating in a competition."

"So what?"

"So I'm going to support her," he said. "I always go and support her."

"You mean you'd put Sue before me?"

He regarded her steadily for a moment. "Now that's a really intelligent thing to say, isn't it?" he said crossly. "Sue's a good friend — to you, too!"

Samantha didn't answer for a moment. "Yes," she said, looking ashamed.

"What?"

"You're right, she is. I'm sorry, of course you must go," said Samantha. "I could do with a few hours practice on my own anyway."

"Oh." Alex looked at her worriedly. "You're sure?" he asked. "Is this really Samantha I hear talking?"

"Yes, it is!" she said. "Now come on, let's make up for it now!"

Saturday found Alex sitting in the auditorium for once, rather than on the ice. He had been there all day long and it felt like it was at least Tuesday.

117

Sue was skating well — she was a good figure skater but everybody knew she wasn't quite good enough to go much higher.

For the first time in hours Alex forgot his freezing feet, for Sue was on the ice, skating as well as he had ever seen her skate before. Every step, every move, every jump, Alex did with her, the adrenalin pulsing around his body. He held his breath as she landed her last double axel and collapsed back into his seat when she finished with a flourish in front of the judges.

He applauded loudly, wishing Toby could be there with his massive voice. Quite a few of the others in the audience joined in with him. Then her marks went up and his mind was battling with the numbers. Yes, she should hold on to third place, better than she'd hoped for. Better than she'd done before, at this level.

It seemed another age before they got to the presentation ceremony and at last the crowd was starting to leave. Thankfully Alex made his way to the anteroom. He had been at the rink since nine o'clock, when the compulsory figures had been skated, and his enthusiasm had been really stretched for the last couple of hours. He switched a smile of congratulation on his face and went in to see the skaters. Sue wasn't there, but Liz, his dance coach, was, and some of the others from the home rink. He had a few words with them all then went in search of Sue. She wasn't anywhere. He tried the coffee bar, the changing rooms, even the car park and he was really getting worried when he heard a muffled sound from behind a row of lockers. Sue was huddled on the floor clasping her knees to her chest, sobbing her heart out.

"Hey, Sue," he said, kneeling down beside her. She shook her head but didn't speak. "You should be celebrating, not crying," he said gently. He put his arms around her. "You knew you couldn't get first place, not with Chrissie Webb entered."

"It's not that," she managed.

"What then?" She wouldn't answer at first, but sat up and wiped her eyes.

"I'll be OK in a minute," she sniffed. "We'd better be getting back. You've got enough problems without mine." She tried to get to her feet but he reached out and stopped her.

"Sue, you've always helped me with my troubles. Now what's wrong?"

She regarded him for a moment, then shrugged. "Brian broke up with me last night."

"Brian did what?" Alex said. Sue had been going out with Brian forever. "Oh, come on, Sue, it was just one of your arguments. He'll be waiting for you when you get back."

She shook her head. "He asked me to choose between him and skating."

"Oh, no," said Alex, depressed.

"He's been getting fed up for ages now. You can hardly blame him. I'm at the rink five nights a week."

"I'm sorry, Sue."

"So am I, Alex," she said. "So very sorry." He put his arms back around her.

"They don't understand, do they? Any of them," he said. "They see us out there for three, four minutes and they think it looks pretty — they never stop to consider what it costs: the training, the social life — oh, everything." He stopped to consider for a second, and added, "I didn't understand it either till Samantha showed me."

Sue blew her nose. "It's worth it though, isn't it, Alex?" It was almost an appeal.

"Oh, yeah," he said, a faraway look in his eyes. "It's worth it!"

16.
The Lucky Ones

"Don't you care?" demanded Toby. "You just wouldn't believe the things that are being said about you and this lunchtime business."

"Ah, it doesn't mean anything," said Alex. "I've got to practice sometime."

Toby was wrestling with the vending machine in the main corridor. He rattled it furiously then gave it a hefty kick but it still refused to relinquish either the chocolate or his change.

"Why doesn't this darned thing ever work?" he said crossly.

"Because people keep kicking it!" said Alex. "Look, do you mind getting a move on? I've a lot to do this lunchtime."

"Don't remind me," said Toby soberly. "Oh, come on then, I just need a quick lift, then you can go and make a fool of yourself."

Toby led the way to the home economics room and he unlocked the door to the pantry. The cake was finally finished and it stood there dominating the whole room, a masterpiece of delicate design. Very carefully they lifted it between them and carried it to the table that had been set up at the front of the room. Delia had suggested that it be displayed there until the wedding, so everybody could see it, as it had been the talk of the school for weeks. As had Alex, dancing in the gym every lunchtime, swathed in an enormous black cloak. He glanced at Toby and sighed at his set expression.

"Look, Toby, Maxie can't help being an idiot! He's just made that way," he said. "If I don't let it get to me, why does it bother you?"

"Because I'm your friend and it rubs off," said Toby. "Anyway, I know it upsets you. I've seen the look in your eyes."

"He's not bothering you, is he?"

"Oh, nothing I can't handle," said Toby. "He's hardly going to try anything physical with me — what's he got to prove by beating me up?"

"Mm," said Alex, looking unhappy. "Listen Toby, if he does bother you, you'd better let me know."

"Why? What are you going to do? Dance round him?" Toby said. "I'd do better going to Hilary — Hilary doesn't take any prisoners!"

"Oh, yes, Hilary," said Alex. "Is that still going on?"

"Certainly it's still going on," said Toby. "We're

going to that new Japanese restaurant on Friday."

Alex smiled. "I might have known," he said. "You know what I said about you not being normal?"

"What about it?"

"Well, you're not!" said Alex. "But when I look at this" — he gestured to the cake — "I can understand a bit more. I mean, to create something like that."

"It's all right," said Toby offhandedly.

"You're kidding? It's perfect!"

"Oh, no," said Toby. "I only wish it was. Look here" — he pointed — "You see that edge there? The marzipan's showing through."

"I can't see anything."

"I can — Hilary can," said Toby. "I'll be honest, if I had the time I'd strip all the icing off and start again."

"No one's going to notice."

"I'll notice," said Toby. "Look, when you're skating, the spectators don't usually notice if you go wrong, do they?"

"They do if you fall down."

"But usually, you manage to cover it, don't you?"

"Of course."

"But it still annoys you — yeah? And you try and make sure it doesn't happen next time?"

"I guess," Alex admitted.

"Well then," said Toby. "We're both artists, Alex. Only with me, when you've finished admiring, you get to eat your mistakes."

Paula Wallace knocked on Mrs. Rollinson's door and at her call went inside.

"Ah, Paula, yes, come and sit down," said Mrs. Rollinson, at her most friendly.

"I'm sorry there's no sign of your curtain," said Paula. "We've looked everywhere."

"Oh well, never mind." Mrs. Rollinson glanced behind her where the one black curtain was now stretched to cover the whole window. "I still can't understand it. Who would want to steal a single curtain?"

"I can't imagine," said Paula, studying her fingernails.

"It disappeared the night of the Valentine's dance," said the Principal. "I'm beginning to think it must have been one of the boys playing the fool. Anyway, I didn't send for you to talk about my curtain. How are you progressing with Samantha Stephens?"

"Very well," said Paula. "She's actually a very nice person when you get through that tough outer shell."

"Oh, yes, I'm sure she is. How about the dancing lessons? Are you coping?"

Paula sighed. "To be honest, it's killing me!"

"I thought you liked dancing?"

"Well, more watching dancing," said Paula. "Oh, I suppose I'm enjoying it, in a masochistic fashion."

"So you think she'll soon start settling in then?"

"Who? Samantha?" said Paula, surprised.

"That *is* who we're talking about, isn't it?"

"Yes, miss, but, I'm sorry, Samantha won't settle in here! There's no chance of that at all."

"Oh, I thought she seemed to be getting along a lot better recently. She goes to lessons. She's taken up swimming — and there's the cycling! I see her on that funny bike of hers every lunchtime, cycling up and down the drive here as if she were practicing for the Tour de France."

Paula sighed. "Her bike's only funny because she's taken the saddle off it," said Paula. "It helps to keep her skating muscles firm. No, Samantha's only waiting until her father gives in. There's no way she's ever going to give up skating."

"And if he doesn't give in?"

"She'll wait until she's sixteen, then run away."

"He'll have her made a Ward of Court."

"Well, she'll wait till she's eighteen then, or thirty, if necessary," said Paula. "I'll be honest, I admire her. I've never met anyone with such strong ambition before."

Mrs. Rollinson laughed. "Paula, if you do go into teaching as you are planning, you will meet others like Samantha," she said. "We've had quite a number here. Not for skating though. We had one girl who did nothing but sit in her room playing her guitar all day — she's in a pop group now. And riding, that's a popular one. We've had quite a few girls who loved horses. Oh, Samantha's not that unusual, a bit stronger than normal perhaps. They're the lucky ones I always think. They know exactly what they're going to do with their lives."

"I'm sorry if this sounds rude, but couldn't you tell her father that?"

"I have," said the Principal. "He's much too worried about her health to listen. You are still taking her temperature before every dance session?"

"Yes. I never miss."

"Good — so, it's just a question of us keeping an eye on her until she sorts things out with her parents?"

"I think so."

"Hm, I see. Well, I might have a quiet word with her mother. She seems more down to earth about Samantha," said Mrs. Rollinson. "Right, now Paula, I asked you to look after Samantha for two months and that time was up a week ago. Do you want to hand her over to another one of the prefects?"

"Oh, no," said Paula hurriedly. "I don't mind at all."

"It's a lot of work, Paula, and your exams are quite soon remember."

"I couldn't walk away from her now."

"Hm — you have to go out with her on Saturdays as well, don't you?"

"Yes, but I love the ballet," said Paula.

"All right then, Paula, if you're sure," said Mrs. Rollinson. Thankfully Paula stood up and opened the door.

"Oh, just a thought, Paula." The Principal stopped her.

"Yes, Mrs. Rollinson?"

"You don't think Samantha could have taken my curtain, do you?"

"Er — no, I don't think so. I mean she's certainly capable of it, especially if it was anything to do with skating. But I can't see what she'd need it for."

17.
Skating into Trouble

Alex held the cloak outstretched as they rounded the end of the ice for the last time. Slowly they came to their dramatic ending, and this time it was perfect. He let the cloak drop and she regarded him, her eyes shining.

"I think that should do," she said quietly.

"It's about time. We've only got one more week," said Alex. "The Juniors is a week this Saturday."

"Ah, but now we know we can do it — it'll work on the day, you'll see," she said. "Now, I think we'd better run through the compulsory dances, don't you? It's all very well winning the free but if we fall down on the compulsories, it'll leave us so far behind we'll never catch up."

"OK, OK," said Alex wearily. He hated the regulation of the compulsories. He undid the cloak and dumped it down by his sports bag.

"Careful," she said. "I want to put it back one day."

"I thought you said it was just some material that no one wanted?" he said.

She deliberately became vague. "I'm not sure those are the exact words I used," she said. Then to change the subject, "Come on, let's cut some ice."

It was Tuesday morning and at last everything seemed to be coming together. The compulsory dances for the Juniors were almost second nature. And now, for the first time, the free dance had felt really good.

They skated for another half an hour and Alex let his momentum take him to a halt by his sports bag.

"Sue will be finished by now," he said. "I want her to watch us run through our free. I mean, we don't really know how it looks, do we?"

Samantha didn't answer. She was staring across the ice to the other side of the rink. Alex followed her gaze. The large girl he'd danced with at the party was standing there with a woman he hadn't seen before.

"Who's the woman?" he asked.

"Mrs. Clarke, the sports teacher," said Samantha.

"Oh, no," he said.

Samantha gave herself a mental shake.

"Alex, I'll have to go over to them. They mustn't see the cloak," she said.

"I'll come with you," he said. Samantha's tough

façade slipped for a moment and she reached for his hand.

"Thanks," she said quietly. Then she sighed, "You can't, Alex. Marella probably hasn't recognized you from this far, she normally wears glasses. If they find out it's you it'll only make more trouble. Look, I'll handle it." Quickly she unlaced her skates and left them with him, then she made her way around the ice. Alex watched her go, a troubled look on his face.

Samantha looked Marella up and down contemptuously. "Nice one, Marella," she said. "You make a real good sneak!"

"Now, Samantha, that's enough of that," said Mrs. Clarke sharply. "Marella didn't know you were here. She's the monitor in charge of the swimming party and she was worried where you'd got to."

"Even you don't believe that," said Samantha.

"I was just doing my job," said Marella.

"Yes, of course you were, Marella," said Mrs. Clarke. "Now you go and gather all the others up."

"Yes, Mrs. Clarke," said Marella demurely.

"I don't get it," said Samantha, when Marella was out of earshot. "How can anyone like her be a favorite of yours?"

"I don't have favorites!" said Mrs. Clarke crossly. "Marella just happens to be a fine athlete."

"A what?" Samantha found this funny. She

shook her head. "Well, come on then, are you going to have me shot at dawn or what?"

"It's not up to me what happens to you," said Mrs. Clarke. She nodded across the ice to where the figure of Alex was still watching. "I take it that that's the boy you've been forbidden to see?"

"What? Oh, him — no! Alex is at my home rink," said Samantha. "I've got boys all over the place. I'm simply not to be trusted."

Mrs. Clarke sighed. "Come on then, Samantha, we'd better be getting back," she said. "Mrs. Rollinson will want to speak to you."

"Something to look forward to," said Samantha bleakly.

The couch in the Barneses' lounge was hard when Alex crept down late that night. He fidgeted, then sat up to look at the time. It was one o'clock. He lay down again knowing he wasn't going to get a wink of sleep, but of course he went out like a light. Fate let him have three whole minutes before the phone, muffled by his pillow, shocked him back to life. Hastily he grabbed for the receiver, the last thing he needed was his parents coming downstairs.

"Sam?" he gasped into the phone.

"The name's Samantha," she said coldly.

"I'm so sorry — I'm not used to being awake this time of night," he said sarcastically. "How was it?"

"Well, I didn't get hung, drawn, and quartered — not quite anyway," she said. "To tell you the truth, Hitler didn't seem that cross — more, oh, I don't know, resigned, I suppose."

"What have they done to you?"

"Oh, detention — stuff like that," she said offhandedly. "I'm grounded, of course, but I was before so that doesn't matter. What does matter is that I'm not allowed out of school *at all*, any more."

"Not even on a Saturday?"

"Nope. I tell you straight, if I was dying they wouldn't even let me go to the hospital."

"Oh." He was silent for a moment while he thought. "So what are we going to do? Forget the competition?"

"We are not!" she said. "You're not serious, after all our work?"

"No, not really," he said. "I was just thinking of you."

"I'll be all right," she said. "Look, Alex, we'll just have to practice on our own all week and hope it works on the day."

"That's what I'm worried about," he said. "How you're going to get out next Saturday."

"I'm digging a tunnel," she said sarcastically. "Oh, I'll manage somehow."

"What about that girl you're friendly with?"

"Paula?"

"That's the one. Did she get into trouble?"

"Why should she?" said Samantha. "She only knew about Saturdays anyway, and she thought they were more to meet you."

"She's a prefect, isn't she?"

"Yes."

"Wasn't she mad?"

"She pretended to be, but she couldn't stop laughing," said Samantha. "Now listen, Alex, I can't stay here too long. The caretaker sometimes walks around late at night."

"Where are you phoning from?"

"Hitler's study."

"The Principal's study?" said Alex incredulously.

"It's the place I know best," she said. "Anyway, I've mailed my costume to Toby, in case it falls into enemy hands. You just make sure you bring it with you on the day."

"Of course," said Alex. "I thought they checked all your mail?"

"They do. I've made friends with the paper boy, he does stuff like that for me," she said. "I think he's got a huge crush on me."

"I'm sure he has," said Alex coldly. "Look, am I going to get any flack from your Principal?"

"Don't think so," said Samantha. "Actually, I think she'll want to keep it quiet, about me getting out that is. It doesn't make her look too good, does it? Don't worry, I'll keep you out of it."

"I didn't mean that," said Alex hastily. "What

I'm thinking is that we don't need my mom and dad trying to stop us from this end, too."

"No," she said. "Look, I'd better go now."

"OK. I can go back to bed then," he said. "When will you call again?"

"We've settled everything, haven't we?"

"Oh — yes," he said. There was a brief silence, then, "I'm not seeing you for ten days then?"

"Eleven, actually."

"OK then, I'll see you in eleven days' time," he said.

"Yeah," she said. "I suppose it'd be an idea to keep in touch — just in case."

"Yes," he said, smiling to himself. "Just in case."

18.
Odds on Alex

Alex and Toby were strolling down the main corridor, arguing as usual. Alex was carrying his cloak and his roller skates bundled up in his arms. It was the morning before the competition.

"You can't miss your sister's wedding," Alex was saying.

"Why not?" Toby demanded. "I don't like her, she doesn't like me. I don't like the jerk she's marrying. I don't like his family, I'm not even that keen on most of my family! Why should I be there?"

"She's your sister."

"I know, I've been trying to live that down for years," sighed Toby. "Besides, I'll be able to make the church. I don't want to miss that if it's at all possible — I want to make absolutely sure she's finally left home!"

"What about the reception? You've got to go to the reception," said Alex.

"I haven't!" Toby shuddered. "I can't stand cold chicken and badly cooked vol-au-vents."

"But you made the cake."

"I'm sure Picasso didn't have to see the public's reaction every time he exhibited a painting," said Toby, completely seriously. "He was quite content knowing he had created a masterpiece."

Alex stopped and faced his friend. "Look idiot, it's just another competition. There'll be plenty more."

"I've never missed a competition yet, I'm not about to start now," said Toby. "Alex, I've just about bust a gut on that antique you call a bike doing your paper route these last months! You don't seriously expect me to miss seeing the end result?"

"I suppose not," sighed Alex. "Thanks, Toby."

"Now don't go getting mushy on me," said Toby. "Tell you what though, you can do me a favor if you want."

"Name it."

"Give the practice session in the gym a rest for today. I've got a double lesson of physics with Maxie, after lunch, and he'll be unbearable after seeing you wearing that darn cloak again."

Alex smiled and shook his head. "Sorry, Toby, can't be done," he said. "It's the last time for a bit though — you can come and watch if you like."

"No, thanks," said Toby hastily. "Anyway, I'm

meeting Hilary. She's having trouble with her filo pastry."

Alex walked away shaking his head. He stopped at the corner and glanced back up the corridor at his friend. "Save a piece of cake for me, Toby," he called.

Toby grinned and headed for the home economics room, his second home. His grin slipped; Maxie was coming towards him. Toby was keeping it from Alex, but he was having real trouble with Maxie lately. Alex seemed impervious to his taunts so he tended to pick on Toby instead.

"Hi, Toby," said Maxie, barring his way.

"Hello, Maxie," Toby sighed. "Get it over with, will you? You insult me, I insult you, then you challenge me to a fight and I'll ignore it, right? Only hurry up, I've got some work to do."

"No — no insults, Toby," said Maxie. "I mean, I still think both you and your friend are first-class wimps, but I'll be honest, I went to see what all the fuss was about this cake of yours, and it's got to be said — it's really something."

"Oh," said Toby, taken aback.

"Yep," said Maxie. "Magnificent — really magnificent." He stepped around Toby and strolled away up the corridor.

Toby stared blankly after him. "The world's going crazy!" he said, shaking his head. Feeling more cheerful he walked on into the home economics room. Hilary was there, an odd expression on her face.

Toby's cake was still sitting in pride of place on the table for all to see, only now there was a large slice out of it.

"Aah — yes, of course," said Toby. He wandered across to survey the damage. Hilary came and put her arms around his shoulders from behind. Toby picked up a small piece of the cake, crumbled it between his fingers, smelled it, and finally put it in his mouth.

"Hm, good texture," he said.

At the same exact moment that Toby was contemplating his ruined cake, Samantha was lying in wait in the locker room. The hockey team was playing a practice match and they would be back soon. At last she heard the familiar loud noise of Marella's voice. Marella wasn't too popular at the moment. Most of the girls were cold towards her because of her actions the week before. They hardly knew Samantha but everybody respected her dedication to skating and the daring way she went about it, and they disapproved of Marella's "tattling" on her.

Marella came striding across, then stopped dead when she found Samantha sitting near her locker.

"What do you want?" she demanded.

"I came to watch you play hockey," said Samantha. "I mean, it looks like I'm going to have to find a new sport, doesn't it?"

"Well, you won't get into the hockey team while I'm captain."

"No," said Samantha. "On second thought I don't really think it's for me. It's not really hard enough. Actually, I find it quite entertaining to watch a bunch of girls with huge bottoms wobbling about all over the place."

"What?"

"I really need something a bit more challenging," mused Samantha, ignoring the storm clouds on Marella's face. "I mean, this sports stuff is all very well but when it comes down to it you're just a lot of school kids playing around, aren't you?"

"You jerk!" Marella found her voice at last. "We've got the best hockey team, the best tennis squad, the best — "

"I'm sure you have." Samantha deliberately yawned.

"I could run rings around you at any sport you could name," said Marella.

"Ah now, that is the problem, isn't it?" said Samantha. "You see, I don't play children's games — like I said, I'm a professional. Tell you what though, back in junior school I used to be red hot at hopscotch — you got a hopscotch team, Marella?"

Marella looked like she was going to attack Samantha but Samantha just sat there smiling sweetly up at her.

"Name it," said Marella through her teeth. "Name any sport, other than skating, and I'll show you."

"We could try a bike race, I suppose," said Samantha.

"You know I haven't got a bike."

"Oh, well, never mind," said Samantha, getting to her feet and stretching luxuriously. She glanced pointedly at Marella's legs. "Pity really, you should be quite good — you've got the thighs for it." She strolled casually to the door.

"You run, don't you?" Marella stopped her. "I've seen you running round the track in a morning."

"Sometimes."

"There's a six-mile road run tomorrow morning," said Marella.

"Is there?" Samantha obviously didn't care.

"You stay with me for a mile — just one mile and I'll, I'll — kiss your feet for you."

"My feet? Oh, well, we are all entitled to our little pleasures," said Samantha. "Anyway, you know I can't — I'm grounded."

"I'll talk to Mrs. Clarke," said Marella. "She's running with us. They'll let you enter if she's there to keep an eye on you."

"Oh, I dunno, it means getting up early, doesn't it?"

"Go on, make my day."

"Well, you have a word with Mrs. Clarke," said Samantha resignedly. "Then we'll see."

The whole school seemed to be gathered around the back of the gym. Even the prefects were there, pretending they weren't prefects. Maxie was standing in the middle of the crowd but as yet there was no sign of Alex.

It was after the end of school and excitement was running high. School fights were usually quick scuffles, a series of half pushes with a bit of wrestling thrown in. A formal challenge behind the gym was rare, and much more serious. Toby was looking worried, he glanced at his watch for the hundredth time. If Alex didn't show it was the total end of his reputation.

Bernie, "The Greek," the school bookmaker was sitting on an upturned trash can, an exercise book open on his knees. Maxie marched over to him.

"What odds are you giving?" he asked aggressively.

"Evens," said Bernie.

"What? The same on him as me?" Maxie said.

"Evens that he turns up," said Bernie.

"Oh — yeah. That sounds about right," said Maxie. "What about if he does? What odds on the fight?"

"I'm offering three to one but there aren't many takers."

"Three to one? You mean on him?" Maxie looked pleased.

"Don't be such a jerk," Bernie sighed. "Three to one on you even surviving, of course."

"You're kidding?" Maxie said crossly. "That's ridiculous!"

"Yeah," Bernie admitted. He considered for a moment then raised his voice. "Seven to two," he called. Maxie gave a snort and pushed away through the crowd. There was a sudden hush and Maxie knew Alex had turned up. Automatically the crowd had moved back to form a circle and Alex walked straight to the center of it where Maxie was waiting. At the sight of him even Maxie's heart began to beat faster.

Alex's face was pure white, his danger signal. Bernie had obviously seen him as well because in the background his voice could be heard raising the odds on Maxie to five to one. Maxie tried to stare Alex out. They hadn't tangled since the sixth grade, and from the ninth grade, that was a lifetime away.

"So you decided to turn up?" he said. Alex didn't answer. Without warning he lifted his hand and slapped Maxie so hard across the face that it knocked him back.

"Aah!" Maxie gasped, holding his face.

"That's so we don't have to waste time," said Alex. "Come on, let's do it."

"Geez," muttered Bernie, impressed. Then

loudly: "Ten to one!" Then, as nobody took up his offer, "Twelve to one!"

Maxie sprang at Alex and at once they were fighting furiously. For no real reason the two boys had always disliked each other. Their fight in the sixth grade had left Alex the victor and Maxie seething with resentment. Then, when Alex had quit the ice-hockey team, for ice dancing, all Maxie's hatred of him had boiled over, and now they were fighting in deadly earnest.

Alex was tall and slim. Maxie shorter and more thick set, but Alex was at the peak of fitness and Maxie felt as though he were punching a plank of wood. Alex, too, was very fast on his feet, circling Maxie, giving two punches for one received. And now Alex had stood up to him, all Maxie's support had drained away and everybody was cheering for Alex.

Maxie was concentrating on Alex's face. Alex tried to keep out of range but he had to come close to get at him. Bang! Bang! Maxie landed two straight punches on the cool, cynical features in front of him but Alex didn't even seem to blink. He came right through Maxie's guard and landed a tremendous drive right on the end of his chin and suddenly Maxie found himself sitting in the dirt.

No one rushed to help him up. He shook his head and struggled to his feet, but it was the end. His guard was down and his blows wild and uncontrolled. Alex backed away waiting his chance, then he ducked a wildly swinging punch and dropped him with a left hook to the side of his chin.

This time Maxie didn't even try to get up. He sat there nursing his jaw, hoping nobody would interfere and help him back into the fight. But no one bothered. They had all fallen silent.

"Finished?" Alex said quietly. Maxie shook his head but it wasn't to say no. Alex dropped his fists and offered Maxie a hand up but Maxie pushed it away, struggled to his feet, and staggered off through the crowd. Everyone started cheering Alex, who was trying to pretend it was all in a day's work. But he couldn't help a grin spreading across his face, even though it hurt to smile.

Toby handed him his jacket without a word and he slipped it on. Bernie shut his book and came over.

"Thanks, Alex," he said. "I wish you'd get into a few more fights, then I could retire. This lot will never learn!" He walked away whistling happily, the only person who had really made a profit from the fight.

Alex finally managed to rid himself of his enthusiastic supporters and disappeared into the locker room. Toby found him there a few moments later, bathing his face with cold water. He glanced at Toby in the mirror.

"Look what that animal's done to my face," he said.

"Mm," said Toby.

"Is that all you can say?" demanded Alex. "What's the matter? You didn't have a bet on Maxie, did you?"

Toby shook his head. "Don't be stupid," he said cheerfully. "Oh, that was beautiful! Pure poetry! That hook to the ribs, the straight punch — then pow! One left hook and it's all over."

"I'm glad you enjoyed it," said Alex. He turned to face his friend. "Look, Toby, I'm sorry about the cake. If I'd seen to Maxie earlier it wouldn't have happened."

"Oh, that," said Toby airily. "That doesn't matter."

"But your sister's getting married tomorrow," said Alex. "What are you going to do?"

Toby sighed. "Alex, you always underestimate me," he said. "I've told you before, I'm a professional."

"So what?"

"Well, a professional always has a second string to his bow." Then, at Alex's baffled gaze, "Look, when the army made the cake for Princess Anne's wedding they didn't make just the one. They had a spare, in case anything happened."

"You mean you've got another one?" Alex demanded.

"Of course," said Toby. "I made one at home

and one at school. Remember I told you I wasn't happy with the icing on the school one? Well, I was planning to share the cake at break time on Monday."

"Oh," said Alex, taken aback.

"Well, I'd better be going," said Toby. "I've a busy day tomorrow: there's your paper route early, then there's the wedding — then your thing."

"Oh, yes, right. I'll see you in the afternoon." Alex said. "Say, Toby, why didn't you tell me about the second cake earlier?"

"Don't be so thick," said Toby. "You wouldn't have had a reason to see to Maxie then, would you? Bye!" Toby gave him a brief smile and went out through the door, leaving it swinging.

19.
Professional Athletes

At six o'clock in the morning it was cold. The breath from the group of girls in front of the main doors misted in front of them. Marella was standing on the tarmac going through a series of bending and stretching exercises, while another handful of girls were standing talking to Mrs. Clarke. At last Mrs. Clarke looked at her watch and clapped her hands.

"It's just about time, girls," she called.

"Samantha Stephens isn't here yet," said Marella.

"We can't wait much longer, Marella," said Mrs. Clarke. "She's probably decided to stay in bed."

"I'll go and haul her out and — " Marella broke off as the front door opened and Samantha came down the steps, dressed in her gray tracksuit.

"Hoping we'd gone?" Marella demanded.

"That's right, Superstar," said Samantha levelly. Mrs. Clarke took her aside.

"Now, Samantha, you've been given permission to go out of the gates, but you're to try and stay with the others — understand?"

"I'll try," said Samantha.

"Yes, but when it gets too much, I shall stay with *you*, not the others — right?"

"Good, I could do with the company," said Samantha. "Shall we get on with it? I'm cold."

Mrs. Clarke gave her an uneasy glance. Then she shrugged and led the girls to the side gate, which she unlocked with her master key.

"OK, girls. It's exactly six miles from here around the course and back to the main gates. The caretaker should have them open for us by that time," said Mrs. Clarke. She glanced at her watch again and put her whistle to her lips.

"Peep!" and they were off. Marella immediately went to the front and set a good surging pace that was designed to take out any beginners. The others ran in a pack just behind her, and Samantha settled in at the back with Mrs. Clarke running alongside.

Samantha was running easily, breathing through her nose. It wasn't true that she was feeling cold, she'd been stretching for the last half an hour in her room. Gradually they strung out, Marella stretching her lead, until at three miles she was some thirty meters ahead. Samantha didn't mind, she was biding her time. At last the sign for a steep hill came up and Marella dug deeper into her reserves as she labored up the incline. This was what Samantha had been waiting for. She sidestepped Mrs. Clarke and accelerated past the pack.

Marella was breathing hard now, her weight telling on the hill, and Samantha passed her like she was standing still.

"Come on, Marella," Samantha urged. "Get those fat legs moving! Show me what a professional athlete is!" Then she was in front and pulling away as though she were in a different gear. Mrs. Clarke, taken by surprise at Samantha's sudden move, came up level with Marella.

"Samantha . . ." she gasped out, but it was pointless, Samantha was almost out of earshot, and they all knew she wasn't going to stop anyway. Marella tried a burst, forcing her tired legs into a sprint but after only fifty meters she staggered off to the side and halted. Mrs. Clarke gave her a reproving glance as she went past.

Samantha shot over the brow of the hill and down the other side. There was an island with four roads off it and waiting at the island was Alex. He was sitting astride his bike and holding Roberta Isgrove's for Samantha.

"Everything OK?" he asked as she came jogging to a halt.

"Fine," she said, taking hold of the bike and

throwing her leg over it. "Why the sunglasses?"

"Disguise," he said as they pedaled off down the London Road. "Did you have any trouble getting away?"

"No," she said. "No trouble at all."

It was four thirty and nervous pairs of skaters were scattered all around the Coliseum. Everybody was waiting while the ice was resurfaced before the free dance competition. Gradually the auditorium was filling up, hardly anybody came to watch the repetitive compulsory dances.

In a corner of the anteroom Alex was sitting in a chair while Sue renewed the makeup that covered the bruises from his fight with Maxie. Samantha was standing watching, a cross look on her face. The door opened and Toby came in eating a hamburger.

"Hey, well done you two," he said. "I've just heard."

"I didn't think you were going to make it," said Alex.

"I've been here for hours," said Toby. "I had to go to the café first, didn't I?"

"Sorry, I wasn't thinking," said Alex.

"I missed my lunch, remember?" said Toby. He turned to Samantha. "How are you, Sammy? How's it feel to be on the run?"

Samantha ignored this. "Look at this moron,"

she said. "They think I'm dancing with a prize-fighter."

"You ought to see Maxie," grinned Toby.

"You might at least have left it till Monday," put in Sue.

"It had waited long enough," said Alex.

"Pity you can't skate in sunglasses, isn't it?" said Samantha caustically. "I wouldn't have minded but you gave me your word you wouldn't get into any fights over me."

"Ah," breathed Toby, understanding at last. "That's why!"

"Yes! So now you know," said Alex. "And you can keep your mouth shut about it."

"I didn't fancy skating with someone who looked like he'd been in a road accident," snapped Samantha. "If I don't mind what Maxie says about me why should you?"

Alex turned to Samantha. "It wasn't over you, it was over something else, right?"

"Keep still," rapped Sue, pushing Alex back in his seat.

"How much longer?" Alex demanded of her. "You put much more on and they won't know which is me and which is Samantha."

"I know about makeup," said Sue. "I've just got the eyes to do."

"No!" said Samantha suddenly. "Leave the eyes."

"You're not serious?" said Sue. "He looks like something that Dracula's just bitten as it is."

Alex turned two magnificent black eyes on Samantha and nodded. "No, she's right," he said. "Leave the eyes."

"All right," sighed Sue. "That's it, then — you're finished."

Alex got to his feet and Sue brushed his pure black costume down with a clothes brush. He stood still as she did so, a resigned expression on his face.

"Was that true?" Samantha demanded of Toby. "About the fight not being over me?"

"Absolutely," said Toby. He grinned. "They had a misunderstanding about a culinary arrangement, that's all."

"Oh," said Samantha, looking put out. Sue noticed the expression on her face and deliberately changed the subject.

"How was the wedding, Toby?" she asked.

"Awful."

"Did your mom cry?" asked Samantha.

"No — she laughed," said Toby. He rubbed his hands together gleefully. "So did I. Just think, she'll never come cluttering up my kitchen again."

Sue finally stood back and regarded Alex. He made quite a startling figure with his white powdered face outlining the somber black eyes.

"You'll do," she said.

"Thanks, Sue," said Alex. He gave her a quick kiss on the cheek.

"You've saved me a seat?" asked Toby.

"Of course," said Alex.

"You're sitting by me and Paula," said Sue.

"Who's Paula?" asked Toby.

"A friend of Samantha's," said Sue. "Now we'd better leave these two alone. They've got to psych themselves up."

It would be at least an hour before Alex and Samantha were on again. They were in first place after the compulsory dances so would be going on last for the free dance. Even so, they needed to start getting their minds in order for the ordeal ahead. They sat close together, not speaking, not even looking at each other, but somehow communicating in that eerie way that only perfect partners can understand. At long last Alex stood up, still without a word, and helped her to her feet. Slowly they made their way down the corridor towards the ice.

"Samantha," a quiet voice said. She gave a start. Her parents were standing at the entrance to the tunnel. There was a long frozen moment until Alex felt he was about to scream, then Samantha ran forward and put her arms around her mother.

"Did you see me skate?" she said quietly.

"Yes, darling. You were wonderful. You were

both wonderful," said Mrs. Stephens. She felt Samantha's forehead. "You're sure you're feeling all right?"

"I'm fine, Mommy, honest," said Samantha. "How did you know I was here?"

"Because I'm your mother, darling," said Mrs. Stephens. "It hardly came as a surprise when Mrs. Rollinson called. We just had to look through a copy of *Skating Times* to find out where you were."

"Oh," said Samantha in a small voice. "And I thought we'd been so clever." She let go of her mother and faced her father. "I'm sorry, Daddy."

He shook his head. "It's all right, sweetheart," he said gently. "Just as long as you're OK."

"You're not going to send me back there, are you?"

"There's not a lot of point, is there?" he smiled. "I don't suppose they'd have you anyway."

"Oh, Daddy!" She ran forward and flung her arms around him.

"Don't cry!" Alex said suddenly, speaking for the first time. "Samantha, you hear me!"

"I'm not," she said in a sniffy voice. "It's just — "

"I couldn't give a darn!" he said, not in his normal character. "Leave it till afterwards! You'll make your eye makeup run!"

Samantha stared at him, and suddenly no one

else existed for them. The bond between them was so strong it was almost a physical force. The bond that was going to take them right to the top.

At last she gave a nod and held out her hand to him.

"Let's do it," she said.

20.
Skating on
the Edge!

The dark, almost awesome figure of Alex stood out in the middle of the ice, alone. The huge cloak was draped around his arms in front of him, his face sunk out of sight in the collar. The crowd craned forward wondering what was happening. There was a dramatic pause and the familiar theme music to *Cloak and Dagger* came over the main speakers, provoking cheers from the younger members of the audience. The music grew louder and louder and still the figure didn't move. Until at last, with the change of tempo, his head came slowly up, the dark eyes standing out startlingly in the glare from the lights. And then he moved, long flowing steps, the cloak billowing out around him. Smoothly he skated the length of the ice and around the far end until finally the arms opened and out of the folds of the cloak appeared the small figure of Dagger, gleaming in her silver costume.

And now everybody's eyes were on her as she

picked up the tempo of the dance, spinning and turning, dodging around but always with Alex just behind her, the black cloak acting as a framework and background for her skating. The music took them around the ice as they explored the theme of the most popular film of the year — the story of two teenage crime-fighters in the Victorian era that had surprisingly caught the imagination of people everywhere and, timed to perfection, whose theme music had just reached number one on the charts.

Their skating speeded up, along with the music, the dance portraying images and feelings — searching for clues, hunting villains, then finally the fight. Cloak picked Dagger up and, with those important side swings, seemed to be using her as a weapon. Then she was back on the ice again dodging and ducking bullets, going down on one skate, turning quickly, until Alex swooped in with his bullet-proof cloak to protect her.

The music reached its searing crescendo taking them back to the middle of the ice, and now everybody who had seen the film knew how it was going to end as Alex enfolded her in the cloak again, and she disappeared from sight leaving him once more standing there, alone.

The crowd, who had been getting a little bored by the other similar free dances, went mad. Toby went even madder, his voice reaching right across the ice.

After a long pause for effect, Alex let her go again and they glided towards the sidelines where Liz, their old coach, was sitting. Not applauding but just sitting there, a contented smile on her face.

Toby was still going strong. Paula looked up at him in embarrassment, then marks went up and she thought he would burst a blood vessel. She dragged him back into his seat.

"Does that mean they've won?" Paula shouted in Sue's ear.

"I should think so," said Sue. "I haven't had time to do the math yet."

" 'Course they've won!" bawled Toby. Paula lost her grip on him and he climbed back up onto his seat again.

Paula picked a handful of peanuts out of her hair where he had scattered them in his excitement. "Does he always behave like this?" she asked Sue.

"Well, usually," smiled Sue. "But you ought to see him when it's a sport he really likes."

In the back row Mrs. Stephens felt for her husband's hand and gave it a squeeze. Back on the ice Samantha was doing exactly the same with Alex. She looked up at him and shouted above the noise of the crowd, "You remember the ending of the film?"

"Eh?" Alex said vaguely. He was trying to pick Toby out in the crowd.

"The ending of the film," she repeated, giving him a shake.

"What about it?" He looked down at her.

"I thought he kissed her."

Alex grinned and shook his head. "No, I don't remember that."

"I'm sure he did," said Samantha innocently.

"Well, I expect you're right — you usually are," said Alex. "I suppose we should try and get the thing true to life."

"That's what I was thinking," said Samantha, linking her hands behind his neck. "Just for the sake of accuracy, of course."

"Yes," said Alex bending forward. "Just for the sake of accuracy."

About the Author

Nicholas Walker was born in the United Kingdom and has managed to do quite a few interesting things. Mr. Walker studied law and banking. He ran clubs and hotels — he even ran a restaurant when he was only twenty-one! At present, he runs a karate club, but he spends his free time cycling, parachuting, ice skating, and writing.

Mr. Walker lives with his wife and two children in Penzance, England.

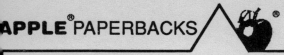

APPLE® PAPERBACKS

Pick an Apple and Polish Off Some Great Reading!

BEST-SELLING APPLE TITLES

❑ MT43944-8	**Afternoon of the Elves** Janet Taylor Lisle	**$2.75**
❑ MT43109-9	**Boys Are Yucko** Anna Grossnickle Hines	**$2.95**
❑ MT43473-X	**The Broccoli Tapes** Jan Slepian	**$2.95**
❑ MT40961-1	**Chocolate Covered Ants** Stephen Manes	**$2.95**
❑ MT45436-6	**Cousins** Virginia Hamilton	**$2.95**
❑ MT44036-5	**George Washington's Socks** Elvira Woodruff	**$2.95**
❑ MT45244-4	**Ghost Cadet** Elaine Marie Alphin	**$2.95**
❑ MT44351-8	**Help! I'm a Prisoner in the Library** Eth Clifford	**$2.95**
❑ MT43618-X	**Me and Katie (The Pest)** Ann M. Martin	**$2.95**
❑ MT43030-0	**Shoebag** Mary James	**$2.95**
❑ MT46075-7	**Sixth Grade Secrets** Louis Sachar	**$2.95**
❑ MT42882-9	**Sixth Grade Sleepover** Eve Bunting	**$2.95**
❑ MT41732-0	**Too Many Murphys** Colleen O'Shaughnessy McKenna	**$2.95**

Available wherever you buy books, or use this order form.

- -

Scholastic Inc., P.O. Box 7502, 2931 East McCarty Street, Jefferson City, MO 65102

Please send me the books I have checked above. I am enclosing $_____ (please add $2.00 to cover shipping and handling). Send check or money order — no cash or C.O.D.s please.

Name_____ Birthdate_____

Address _____

City_____ State/Zip _____

Please allow four to six weeks for delivery. Offer good in the U.S.A. only. Sorry, mail orders are not available to residents of Canada. Prices subject to change.

APP693

APPLE *Classics*

❏ MA43389-X	**The Adventures of Huckleberry Finn**	Mark Twain	**$2.95**
❏ MA43352-0	**The Adventures of Tom Sawyer**	Mark Twain	**$2.95**
❏ MA42035-6	**Alice in Wonderland**	Lewis Carroll	**$2.95**
❏ MA44556-1	**Anne of Avonlea**	L.M. Montgomery	**$3.25**
❏ MA42243-X	**Anne of Green Gables**	L.M. Montgomery	**$2.95**
❏ MA43053-X	**Around the World in Eighty Days**	Jules Verne	**$2.95**
❏ MA42354-1	**Black Beauty**	Anna Sewell	**$3.25**
❏ MA44001-2	**The Call of the Wild**	Jack London	**$2.95**
❏ MA43527-2	**A Christmas Carol**	Charles Dickens	**$2.75**
❏ MA45169-3	**Dr. Jekyll & Mr. Hyde: And Other Stories** of the Supernatural	Robert Louis Stevenson	**$3.25**
❏ MA42046-1	**Heidi**	Johanna Spyri	**$3.25**
❏ MA44016-0	**The Invisible Man**	H.G. Wells	**$2.95**
❏ MA40719-8	**A Little Princess**	Frances Hodgson Burnett	**$3.25**
❏ MA41279-5	**Little Men**	Louisa May Alcott	**$3.25**
❏ MA43797-6	**Little Women**	Louisa May Alcott	**$3.25**
❏ MA44769-6	**Pollyanna**	Eleanor H. Porter	**$2.95**
❏ MA41343-0	**Rebecca of Sunnybrook Farm**	Kate Douglas Wiggin	**$3.25**
❏ MA45441-2	**Robin Hood of Sherwood Forest**	Ann McGovern	**$2.95**
❏ MA43285-0	**Robinson Crusoe**	Daniel Defoe	**$3.50**
❏ MA42323-1	**Sara Crewe**	Frances Hodgson Burnett	**$2.75**
❏ MA43346-6	**The Secret Garden**	Frances Hodgson Burnett	**$2.95**
❏ MA44014-4	**The Swiss Family Robinson**	Johann Wyss	**$3.25**
❏ MA42591-9	**White Fang**	Jack London	**$3.25**
❏ MA44774-2	**The Wind in the Willows**	Kenneth Grahame	**$2.95**
❏ MA44089-6	**The Wizard of Oz**	L. Frank Baum	**$2.95**

Available wherever you buy books, or use this order form.

Scholastic Inc., P.O. Box 7502, 2931 East McCarty Street, Jefferson City, MO 65102

Please send me the books I have checked above. I am enclosing $_____ (please add $2.00 to cover shipping and handling). Send check or money order — no cash or C.O.D.s please.

Name _____

Address _____

City _____ State/Zip _____

Please allow four to six weeks for delivery. Available in the U.S. only. Sorry, mail orders are not available to residents of Canada. Prices subject to change.

AC1092